ALIEN BATTALION

Eric S Brown

Special Military Advisor- Kevin W. Pierce

SEVERED PRESS
HOBART TASMANIA

ALIEN BATTALION

ALIEN BATTALION

The dropship rattled as she roared downwards through the atmosphere of Qacov IV. Corporal Laybourne was used to it. This was far from his first rodeo. Atmospheric stress on a ship's hull was nothing. He was more concerned with the sound of the detonating ordinance the Kep'at forces on the ground below were filling the sky with.

Laybourne glanced around at the other members of his platoon. First Lieutenant Gira's face was like stone. He, too, knew what was coming in the next few moments. Sergeant Dixon appeared to be taking a nap, slouched over against his safety harness. Whether he really was or was just faking it, Laybourne could never tell.

So many of the other faces surrounding him in the rear of the dropship, were new ones. The Hell's Banshees had taken heavy losses during their last mission. Over forty percent battalion wide from what he'd heard. Finding replacements was never difficult. Finding good ones was. Every kid who could hold a gun with romantic dreams of war and glory, every criminal dodging the "law," every failed colonist in debt and without a penny to their name, every suicidal freak looking for a quick way to die, came out in force wherever and whenever the Hell's Banshees put out word it was offering employment.

Laybourne was glad his job was simple. Point the end of his rifle at the "bad guys" and pull the trigger. He didn't have to sort through all the losers who wanted to be a part of the Hell's Banshees and determine who was worthwhile and who would only get those around them killed. Besides, he had been one of those losers himself not too long ago.

He felt the dropship shift, its end tilting upwards, as it came in hard and fast to touch the surface of Qacov IV. The thud of its landing gear making contact echoed through the rear of the vessel. Everyone inside the ship could hear small arms' fire pinging against its hull.

"What ya hear, newbies?" Sergeant Dixon yelled, snapping awake.

"Nothing but the rain!" Coyote Platoon responded in chorus.

Laybourne flinched as the dropship's rear door blew to allow Coyote Platoon's exit from her. Sergeant Dixon led the charge out of the ship and was immediately cut to pieces. High velocity rounds tore through his hardened battle armor to splatter his blood and guts over the men behind him. Several other troops went down before Coyote Platoon was able to open up with enough return fire to reduce the amount that was being leveled on them.

Everything became a blur to Laybourne as he cleared the dropship's exit and broke right, running for cover. The ship had touched down just outside the city of Za'l. The road leading into the city was cluttered with abandoned land vehicles and the wrecked, burnt-out hulls of Qacovian tanks. Even with the sheer number of Banshee troops the dropships had deposited on the ground, the city defenders' fire was too hot to charge them.

A burst of rounds hissed through the air so close to Laybourne's head, that he threw himself to the dirt and began to crawl the rest of the way towards the remains of the closest Qacovian tank on his belly. He could hear rounds pinging off the other side of the wreckage as he raised himself into a crouch. His knuckles were white from the pressure of the grip he clutched his rifle with. It took him a moment to realize he wasn't alone. Marcus was hunched up against the side of the tank next to him. Laybourne could tell at a glance, Marcus had been hit.

Marcus must have noticed the expression on his face because he growled, "Hurts like Hell. Had worse though."

From how Marcus's hand was pressed against his side and the amount of blood that seeped through and over his gloved fingers, Laybourne doubted it.

Two Banshee strike craft screeched through the air above them, making a run at the city.

"At least we got air support on this one," Laybourne shrugged.

Explosions shook the ground as the strike craft ripped the Kep'at troops inside the city gate a new one. Laybourne knew he needed to move. There was nothing he could do for Marcus. He wasn't a medic.

"Go on, man," Marcus urged him, knowing what he must be thinking.

Laybourne gave up his cover and charged towards the city gate. As he ran, his legs pumping under him, he saw that the gate had already fallen. Banshees were pouring through it. The only fire coming at them now was from a few Kep'at troops who still held the high ground of the city's walls.

He plunged through the shattered gateway into the city in the wake of several other Banshees. It was like stepping into Hell. Banshee troops and Kep'at forces were everywhere. Firefights raged all around him. Laybourne didn't want to get bogged down in the chaos himself. Someone needed to reach the planetary shield control center in the center of the city. The faster that place was reduced to rubble, the faster all this would be over.

Hell's Banshees held a vast advantage over the Kep'at forces on Qacov IV. The Kep'at forces were nothing more than a few garrisons, like the one here, scattered around the planet. If Qacov IV's shield was taken down, there was nothing to stop *The Hellhound*, which was the battalion's base ship in orbit, from ending this madness in a matter of minutes. Even Kep'ats would back down if they knew you had the means to nuke them from orbit. *The Hellhound* sure did. She was one of the biggest ships owned by any Merc company like the Hell's Banshees in known space. She was part destroyer and part carrier with some serious teeth. Colonel Hell had invested a lot in her. The *HellHound's* size and firepower made her a force to be reckoned with.

Corporal Laybourne darted down a side street, partly seeking to escape from the primary combat zone and partly in search of a clear towards the center of the town where the shield station was positioned. The alley was deserted. He paused when he reached its other end, pressing his back flat against one of the walls at the mouth of its exit to peer into the street beyond. He could see the shield station from his position. His path to it was blocked by Kep'at soldiers scrambling out of it to reinforce those locked in combat with the Hell's Banshee forces at just inside the city gates. He jerked his head back, wanting to remain unseen. All he had to do was get across the street and toss the package he was carrying into the station. On a normal day, he would've been leading Fire Team Bravo but today, he was alone. Each of the Banshee dropships carried a designated runner whose sole purpose was to reach the shield station and blow it. He had drawn the short stick for his ship before the drop and the job had become his.

The battle at the city gates had drawn most of the Kep'at troops to it, making his job easier. Laybourne knew better than to simply rush the shield station like some sort of hero in a comic book. Heroics in real life got you dead real fast.

Holding his breath until the squads of Kep'at rushing for the gates were past his position, Laybourne waited for his moment to come. He couldn't see any other Banshee troops near the shield station. It might be that he was the only runner who made it through and if so, he had to make his next move count.

Laybourne poked his head around the corner of the alley again to scan the outside of the shield station. The building was a small one. He doubted there could be many Kep'at left inside it. No, the danger came from the A.I.-controlled gun turrets atop the building. They would cut him to pieces before he was halfway across the street to his target. He popped an EMP grenade from his belt and activated it by giving its top section a half twist.

Aiming his throw carefully, Laybourne sprang from the alley and lobbed the grenade directly at the front of the shield station. The A.I.-driven turrets opened up in his direction as he dove back into the alley. The walls at the alley's mouth were torn to shreds by their fire, chunks of shattered wood and concrete exploded over him as he hit the dirt. He heard the whine of the EMP grenade detonating. The pitch of the whine grew and then peaked into a shrill whistle-like noise. The fire of the enemy gun emplacements fell silent. He got to his feet, risking another look outside the alley. The guns slumped on their turrets, powered down by the EMP blast.

Laybourne dove out of the alley, running as fast as he could towards the shield station. He unslung the heavy backpack he carried on his shoulders and swung it in the air over his head. Releasing the pack at just the right angle, he sent it flying to land just outside the shield station's main entrance. His job done, he whirled about, racing once more for cover.

As he did so, he heard the gun turrets powering back up. He cursed as they opened fire at him again. A stream of rounds cut a path of flying dust on the ground behind him, closing in on him as he ran. He knew he wasn't going to reach the alley in time even before the first round that hit him entered his right leg from behind and exited its front in a shower of blood. The warm, wet liquid splashed over the ground as Laybourne went down.

Screaming, he tumbled into the dirt, fighting not to try to clutch his wounded leg. The fact that his momentum kept him moving despite the fall was the only thing that saved his life. He rolled to the left as the stream of fire continued on along his previous path.

The gun turrets suddenly stopped firing as the world around Laybourne went white.

****

Corporal Laybourne opened his eyes. He felt like he was drifting on a cloud, the haze of its white mists obscuring the clarity of his senses. It took some time for him to realize he was in one of the *Hellhound's* sickbays. The euphoria he was experiencing was no doubt caused by the amount of painkillers the auto-doc had pumped him full of while it had worked on his wounded leg. Laybourne was glad to see that the leg remained attached to his body. The hole blown through his leg by the round from the Kep'at gun turret had left it hanging on by little more than strands of muscle and sinew. On his homeworld, such a wound wouldn't have left any chance of the leg being able to be saved, but the *Hellhound's* medical tech was the best that money could buy and a mish-mash of tech from all around known space. Colonel Hell knew that taking care of trained troops was a better investment than simply hiring replacements.

The sick bay was full of other wounded Banshees. Across from where he lay, he saw a Gimak Banshee with his green-skinned chest open, ribcage pulled apart along its sternum. An auto-doc unit hung from the ceiling above the Gimak, performing some kind of procedure on the unconscious man. Gimaks were tough by nature. Over the years, Laybourne had fought side by side with a fair number of them. A male Gimak had three hearts, if he recalled correctly, and the auto-doc looked hard at work on saving all three of them. The Gimak Banshee had taken a blast to his chest that had not only penetrated his armor but almost turned the bulk of the insides of his upper torso to pulp. It was a miracle that Gimak was even alive for the auto-doc to work on.

"It was a mess down there, son," a man sitting beside Laybourne's bed said, snapping the corporal's attention around to him. Laybourne nearly jumped up from his bed as he saw the man was Sergeant Major Page.

"At ease, Corporal," the Sergeant Major barked at him. "You may not be as bad off as Lieutenant Calibar over there, but that doesn't mean you should be getting yourself worked up."

"Yes, sir," Laybourne answered, trying to force his nerves to relax. He knew who the sergeant major was and had seen him around before, but the two of them had never met face to face as they were now. Sergeant majors usually didn't waste their time with mere corporals unless something was seriously wrong. Laybourne didn't even know what to say to the sergeant major. Page was second-in-command of the Banshees, answerable only to the colonel himself. The sergeant major also had a rep of coming down like a hammer on anyone who broke the rules of the Banshees. In addition to being second-in-command, Page was also the colonel's personal hitman.

"You're not in trouble, Corporal," Page told him, apparently seeing the fear in his eyes. "Rather the opposite, son. You were the only one of our runners who made it through to the Kep'at shield station down there. If it hadn't been for you, we'd all still be slugging it out with those bastards."

Laybourne stared at Sergeant Major Page. Page was a human too, but his body was misshapen from years of worth of enhancements and combat damage repairs. Page's head seemed too small for the massive shoulders it rested on. Seeing Page up close was very different than catching a glimpse of the man across a hangar bay or at the other end of a dropship's troop compartment. Labeling Page human might be an overstatement these days even if the man had started out as one. Even the fingers of his hands were a mix of metal and flesh. His right hand sported three robotic digits and on his left, his thumb and pointer finger resembled metal pincers much more than anything human in nature. This up-close look at the sergeant major certainly added credence to the stories of just how strong the man was rumored to be.

At last, Laybourne found the professional courage to speak up. "How can I help you, sir?"

Page smiled, stretching back the chair by Laybourne's bedside. The chair creaked from the weight of his mass shifting in it, straining to hold together.

"The colonel and I were deeply impressed by your actions, son." Page's grin turned almost feral. "You see, we're looking for someone to take on a very special op for the Banshees and we both agree that you might just be the person we've been looking for."

Laybourne's guts churned in his stomach. He had been a Banshee long enough to know special ops often went hand in hand with what most would actually label suicide missions.

"The Kep'at have been pushing farther and farther into Alliance space. So far, the Earth Alliance has cut those bastards a lot of a slack, leaving it up to independent Merc units like us to deal with their incursions, at least on the worlds that can afford our services. Things are coming to a head though, son, and the Alliance may have no choice but to deal with the Kep'at head on in an outright war. If that happens, there are those who believe the Alliance will lose," the sergeant major explained.

"Lose, sir?" Laybourne asked in disbelief. The Earth Alliance was the most powerful in known space. It was light years ahead of the Kep'at in terms of tech and its navy was second to none.

"Did you not hear me, son?" the sergeant major growled. "Do they have you too doped up for you to understand Galactic Standard?"

"No, sir," Laybourne answered quickly.

"Colonel Hell has it on good authority from contacts he has inside the upper command structure of the Alliance's military that the Kep'at have made contact with a new race beyond the galactic rim. If the rumors regarding this race's strength, in terms of numbers, is to be even halfway believed, we're all in some serious trouble," Page went on. "They could sweep through Alliance space like a swarm of locusts devouring everything in their path."

Page paused before continuing, "I know what you're thinking, son. Trust me, I do. I didn't want to believe any of this either when the colonel briefed me on the situation either. Truth is, though, these new allies of the Kep'at are very real and we need to know all we can about them before they can bring the bulk of their forces to bear on the Alliance."

"And the Earth Alliance hired the colonel and us Banshees to find out what we can about this race before they make their move," Laybourne ventured and then hastily added, "sir."

"Exactly." Page grinned in a manner that sent shivers down Laybourne's spine. "That's where you come in, Corporal, or should I say, First Lieutenant Laybourne?"

Laybourne swallowed hard. "Thank you, sir."

"My pleasure, Lieutenant Laybourne," the major nodded. "Colonel Hell wants to brief you on your mission personally as soon as you're cleared for duty. Report to his office at that time."

"Yes, sir," Laybourne saluted Major Page as the senior officer stood.

"Good luck, Lieutenant," Page said before heading for the sickbay's exit.

Laybourne heard the man mumbled something that sounded like "You're gonna need it," on his way out. He sighed and sat staring up at the ceiling above him. As if talking with the major wasn't terrifying enough, coming face to face with Colonel Hell under even the best circumstances was any Banshees' worst nightmare. Laybourne almost wondered if he should get his gun and shoot himself in his other leg.

****

Auto-docs were wonderful tools but they were just that, tools. When it came to decisions about whether or not a wounded Banshee could return to active duty, those rested with the battalion's four doctors. Dr. Worley, a fellow human, was handling Laybourne's case. It had taken the doc two days after the surgery to admit that Laybourne was ready for duty again. That had been fine with Laybourne. New rank or not, lying in sickbay and being taken care of was better than being at the sharp end of things any day. His upcoming meeting with Colonel Hell had weighed heavily on his mind during those two days and there was no denying he was dreading it. Laybourne was a veteran and confident in his ability to get a job done. He was no stranger to command either, having been a corporal for over a year before his sudden promotion to lieutenant. Handling a fire team was an up-close and personal thing, though and he imagined the colonel was going to be dumping a lot more on him than even he expected if he told himself the truth.

His orders were to report to the colonel once he was declared fit for duty, but the major hadn't said he couldn't stop by his quarters to get cleaned up first. Quarters aboard the *Hellhound* usually accommodated a squad of four and he shared this with his fire team, a Gangly named Leon and a Mezzonite named T'chal, assuming they had survived the cluster frag that had been Qacov IV. Their fourth roommate, Rigal, had died during the team's previous op and they were still waiting for someone else to be assigned to them. Laybourne assumed his quarter's assignment would be changing with his new rank, but for the time being, all his stuff was still where he had left it.

Leon lay in one of the quarter's bunks, an old-fashioned book held in his hands, reading as the door of the quarters slid open to admit Laybourne. T'chal was there too, playing solitaire with the deck of cards Laybourne had given him a few weeks back. T'chal had caught on quick to the game when Laybourne taught it to him and it had since become close to an addiction for the Mezzonite. Both of them looked up at Laybourne as stepped through the doorway and then suddenly snapped to attention at the sight of the new rank he wore on his uniform.

"At ease, guys," Laybourne said. "We've known each other too long to get bent out of shape over rank when we're off duty."

T'chal grabbed him up in a bear hug that nearly caused Laybourne's ribs to cave in on themselves. "Glad to see you alive! It is happy greeting time!" T'chal roared.

"Easy there, big guy!" Laybourne yelled struggling against the painful hold T'chal held him close in.

T'chal released him, taking a step back. Mezzonites weren't known for their intelligence so much as they were their brute strength and stone-like skin. They were short bipeds, similar to humans in shape but much more dense and burly. T'chal's yellow eyes looked at him with guilt.

Laybourne rubbed at his aching ribs. "I'm okay, T'chal," he assured the Mezzonite. "It's good to see you too. They didn't tell me if you guys had made it through alive or not."

Leon gave a half chuckle, his lips twisted into a smug sort of smirk but said nothing. The Gangly was everything that T'chal wasn't. Superhumanly fast and agile, Laybourne had once seen

Leon take down five other Banshees in a barroom brawl before the others had been able to do much more than bark a threat at him. His matching daggers hung from the belt around his waist and Laybourne had never seen Leon take them off except to bathe.

"What brings you by, Lieutenant?" Leon asked coldly. Laybourne was used to his tone and didn't take offense from it. Gangly culture was a warrior one, and though he knew Leon respected him and perhaps even considered him a friend in his own way, to expect a warm welcome from the Gangly would be like expecting a blue sky on Earth to rain blood on the green fields below it.

"Need a shave. Apparently, I have a meeting with Colonel Hell." Laybourne fetched his razor from the drawers under his bunk and headed for the room's bath section.

"What did you do, you poor human thing?" T'chal asked. Even Leon cocked an eyebrow at Laybourne's confession.

"Too good at my job, I reckon," Laybourne answered.

"I will say a prayer for you, sir," Leon nodded at him and then returned to his own bunk to resume his reading.

"Corporal Laybourne can't be executed," T'chal boomed. "He has done nothing wrong."

"It's first lieutenant now, T'chal," Laybourne reminded the Mezzonite gently as he began shaving. "And the colonel's not going to execute me, T'chal. He just wants to brief me on my next op."

"If the colonel is involved, is that not same thing?" T'chal replied, a deep sadness in his gravel like voice.

"Let's hope not, T'chal," Laybourne said. "Let's hope not."

****

Two heavily armed Banshee troopers stood outside the door of the colonel's office as Laybourne approached it. He tried to hide the fact that every nerve in his body felt frayed from the stress of the meeting that was waiting on him on the other side of the door.

The guards stopped him and ran through a routine of checking him for weapons. His identification was confirmed via a quick DNA scan by a prick on his right pointer finger.

"You're cleared, sir," the larger of the two guards told him. "You can go in now. The colonel is expecting you."

Laybourne nodded politely at the guards. He couldn't help but notice that both of them were human. The Banshees had at least a hundred aliens in their ranks with various bio-talents. Some were stronger than humans, others faster, still others smarter. Heck, some of them could even do weird things like read minds. And yet, every one of the colonel's personal guards he had encountered during his time with the Banshees was human. That struck Laybourne as odd. He couldn't help but wonder why? Did the colonel see some trait in humanity that the other races were missing? If so, what was it? He didn't have time to dwell on the question no matter how much it piqued his curiosity. One did not keep Colonel Hell waiting.

The door to office slid open to allow him to enter. Laybourne stepped inside. The office was dark and very spacious. Its entire rear wall was a giant window into the stars. He couldn't tell if the vacuum and coldness of space was held back some sort of hardened glass or an energy field. Whatever it was made of, it was too transparent to even guess at.

There was only a single desk in the office, just a hair closer to the giant window than the room's center. The colonel's chair sat vacant behind it and two empty chairs were positioned in front of the desk. There were no extra guards inside the office which was surprising to Laybourne. Someone like Hell didn't get where they were by not taking every possible precaution.

Colonel Hell stood across the room from its entrance with his back to Laybourne. The colonel appeared to be staring out into the ocean of stars outside the *Hellhound's* armored hull.

"You wanted to see me, sir," Laybourne said.

The colonel turned to face him. He looked nothing like the legends painted him to be. And oh were there legends. Laybourne had lost count of the stories he had heard since joining the Banshees about the colonel. They ranged from the flat-out impossible to the merely incredible. There were stories of the colonel taking out an entire platoon of Kep'at, alone and unarmed. There were stories of just how cold the man was and how he had once nuked an entire planet from orbit, civilians included, because the governor of the planet had insulted his honor. Others claimed the man once risked his own life and that of every Banshee under his command to save a single child that had survived on a world the Kep'at had ravaged. Those stories were in the minority, however. Most spoke of the colonel's coldness and adeptness at killing. Looking at the colonel, Laybourne could see why.

Colonel Jerimiah Hell wasn't a human. Though his body shape was that of a well-toned, human male in early thirties, his skin was a greenish blue. He was short, too, by human standards, to be such a figure of legend, standing only five feet and eight inches tall. His hair was midnight black atop his head and neatly cut to Banshee regulation standards. He wore his rank on the sleeves of his perfectly fitted, black uniform. Even here, in the safety of his own office, Colonel Hell wore a sidearm holstered on his right hip. The features of his face were finely chiseled and almost bird like. His lips were a darker blue than the skin surrounding around and his nose, though human in form, protruded ever so slightly like a beak. He moved with a cat-like grace as he walked towards Laybourne. Each movement filled with the confidence of a man who had seen death and bested it many times over. There was a lethal air about him that very clearly expressed that one never wanted to get on his bad side.

The most striking thing about the colonel, however, was his eyes. They glowed a bright green in the dim light of the office. Their orbs contained no pupils or irises. Instead, they resembled miniature stars trapped within their sockets. He could see a keen intelligence lurking behind their gaze as it fell upon him. It felt as if they cut deep into his soul and maybe even beyond it.

No one knew what race the colonel belonged to. There was no other like him in known space. Some believed he was the last of his kind, alone among the stars with only his battalion of Banshees as his clan. Others believed he had never been born but rather had been created by the Alliance as an instrument of war and had somehow escaped or earned his freedom to go into business for himself.

"Thank you for coming so quickly, First Lieutenant Laybourne," Colonel Hell purred. His voice was soft and not much more than a whisper though it seemed to echo across the office as the colonel spoke. "We have much to discuss."

Laybourne stood at attention, waiting for Colonel Hell to continue.

"You've been a Banshee for several years now, Lieutenant," Hell said. "In that time, I have never once received a discipline complaint against you. That alone sets you apart from most of the Banshees you share this ship with."

"Thank you, sir," Laybourne snapped out the words.

The colonel raised one of his hands, running the tip of his thumb over its pinky finger. "Your combat record is impressive as well to an extent."

Pausing, the colonel gave him a sideways look. "You *are* in the Banshees, however, so I do not mean that is impressive in regards to your number of survived drops or enemy kills. No, Lieutenant, what impresses me about you goes deeper than that. You put the job ahead of everything else. When something needs to be done, you find a means no matter the cost. This latest operation on Qacov IV is proof of that."

"This one was just dumb luck, sir," Laybourne spoke up.

Colonel Hell shook his head. "I think it was more than that. I watched you from the *Hellhound,* First Lieutenant. Whether you realize it rationally or not, each step you took from the moment you dove out of that dropship was a calculated one. It was your focus and determination that carried you through the city to that shield station, not dumb luck as you say. Your actions saved us a lot of lost personnel and ended the conflict on Qacov IV faster than perhaps even I was able to foresee."

Laybourne didn't know how to respond to such a compliment so stayed silent.

"The Banshees are your family, Lieutenant Laybourne, any fool can see that but there was more to actions on Qacov IV than just that which pushed you on, wasn't there?"

"Yes, sir," Laybourne admitted, hoping he wouldn't get a bullet in the head for doing so. "I was born on a world like Qacov IV. I know what it's like to have your home taken over by an alien force and not know if you'll live another day under it."

Colonel Hell snapped his thumb against the middle finger of the hand he had held up, grinning. "That's why it has to be you."

"Excuse me, sir?" Laybourne asked. "I don't understand."

"You're a killer, Laybourne, tried and true. Cold enough to do what needs doing but also still human enough to have compassion about those caught in the crossfire. Above all, I believe you're loyal to a fault."

"*Hellhound,* show us the Ventari system," Colonel Hell ordered. Immediately, the window into space shifted into a galactic map. Its view zoomed in on the system the colonel had named. It sat on the edge of Alliance space, bordering the Kep'at Free State. No name could be more misleading in what it conveyed, Laybourne thought. The Kep'at were known throughout space as the most brutal slavers and their government ruled its citizens with an iron fist. The view continued to close in on a single planet, seventh in orbit around the system's oversized sun.

"That is Ventari VII," Colonel Hell told him. "It's where you'll be heading to when our chat here is done. It's also the world that I and several higher ups in the Alliance military believe will be the initial target of attack for the Kep'at's new allies. I am sure Sergeant Major Page briefed you on them."

"Not much, sir," Laybourne said.

"That's because we know so very little at this point in time, First Lieutenant. Your job is to take a company of my Banshees there and find out exactly what we're up against before they hit Alliance space in force."

Laybourne realized his mouth was hanging open and closed it. "A company, sir?" he stammered.

"An undersized one, yes. I'm giving you one hundred men, a mech unit, and three very costly tanks, First Lieutenant. Sergeant Richards will be your second-in-command. Despite his rank, he's a man I trust. He's survived ten times the number of drops you have, so I recommend you listen to whatever wisdom he shares with you."

"Yes, sir!" Laybourne snapped.

Colonel Hell gave his reply a dismissive wave. "Ventari VII is not an Alliance world. Its location has made it untenable for colonization. Thus far, the Kep'at have left it alone as well. That is not to say it isn't a populated one. Alliance probes confirm that there is a small civilization upon it, albeit a low-tech one by our standards. At best, the probes place the world's tech level at one roughly equivalent to that of your homeworld's, Earth, a few decades passed your race's third World War. Part of your job will be to make contact with the world's populace and see if they are open to working with us against the Kep'at. Having their natives forces with you could make a difference if things come to a head before the *Hellhound* arrives for your extraction, and trust me, she'll be coming in hot when she does. We want you to engage these new allies of the Kep'at with everything you have at your disposal. Feel them out if you will. There will be only a narrow window in which we *can* get you and your men out. The Alliance isn't paying us enough to make a stand at Ventari VII. They're paying us for intel. Again, that, above all, is the primary focus of your mission."

"And this native population, sir?" Laybourne asked, not wanting to hear the answer. "Am I to consider them expendable?"

"If they are amenable to a treaty with the Alliance, you can certainly help them apply for one but you and I both know that the Alliance isn't going to spend its ships defending a world so easily written off. That said, anything you can do to help them fight back, hurt the Kep'at's new allies, well, by all means. . ."

The view screen shifted back into a window looking out at the stars as the two men's "chat" came to an end.

"Any other information you may need will be in your orders, First Lieutenant Laybourne. I expect your company to away and in route to Ventari VII before twenty-three hundred hours."

"Will that be all then, sir?" Laybourne asked.

Colonel Hell laughed. His laughter stung Laybourne's ears like fingernails dragging along the length of an old Earth chalkboard. "Just don't screw this one up, Laybourne. Too many people are counting on you, I among them."

"I won't, sir," Laybourne said and headed for the office's door.

****

The *Cerebus*'s engines roared to life as she lifted out of the *Hellhound*'s gigantic port hangar bay. She was no small ship herself, yet the *Hellhound* held seven more like her within its bays. Technically, she was classed as a transport, more than capable of carrying the company of Banshees, mechs, and tanks Laybourne had been assigned, but she had teeth. The *Cerebus* was armed with forward beams weapons as well as forward and aft missile launchers. A true battleship would tear her to shreds, but against anything less, she could hold her own. No pirate in their right mind would ever think of coming after her. More importantly, she was built tough enough to enter a planet's atmosphere herself and set down on its surface. The *Cerebus* was a mobile base for the Banshees she carried and Laybourne was glad to have her.

Her Captain, Pulliman, seemed capable and that helped put Laybourne at ease. As at ease as he could be with so much resting on his shoulders. Part of him wished he had stood up to Colonel Hell and refused this mission. To say it was out of his league would be the understatement of the eon as he saw things. Still, the colonel had faith in him. Hell had just given him near a tenth of the Banshee's overall strength to command and one of the Banshee's eight transports. Not to mention the three state-of-the-art tanks that sat in the *Cerebus*'s hold.

Captain Pulliman and his crew navigated the *Cerebus* away from the *Hellhound*. She had to be a good distance from the Banshee's command ship before she could make her FTL jump to Ventari VII. FTL travel was not something that Laybourne was a fan of. It was a part of the job he just had to endure. An FTL jump left everyone aboard out of whack for a few moments after it occurred, even trained ship personnel like Pulliman and his crew. For ground pounders like Laybourne, that out-of-whack feeling often lead to emptying one's guts on the floor and seeing your last meal half-digested in front of you. There were drugs to help with the effect of FTL travel, but Laybourne was allergic to them.

An FTL jump had to be carefully calculated or a ship and her crew could just as easily find themselves blinking back into existence inside a star or the event horizon of a quantum singularity. Laybourne was a whiz at basic math but when it came to the kind of number crunching required for an FTL jump, he couldn't even pretend to understand the equations.

Laybourne did his best to stay clear of Captain Pulliman and his crew as they went about their preparations. He figured the last thing that they needed was a nervous mess of an officer breathing down their necks while they worked. He had served under officers like that and promised himself he wasn't going to be one.

"All systems are green, sir," Captain Pulliman reported. "We're ready to jump when you give the word."

Laybourne had spent the hours while his men got assembled and their gear was loaded onto the *Cerebus* reading everything he could about Ventari VII in the reports that Colonel Hell had given him. He knew barely anything more than he had known before he started. His gut told him this mission had to be handled carefully. The population of the planet could prove key in his strategy to engage and reconnoiter the Kep'at's new allies when they decided to show themselves.

"And you're sure we won't be detected by the planet's populace when we jump in system?" Laybourne asked.

Captain Pulliman nodded. "Our cloak will be fully engaged. It's extremely unlikely based on the information we have that anyone on that planet will be able to detect us even with our engines at maximum power."

"Good," Laybourne said, appraising Pulliman once more. The man really did seem to know his stuff. "I want us into orbit as quickly as possible and detailed scans of the planet commenced at once. We'll need to find a nice, scenic place to sit down where we won't be discovered."

"Understood, Lieutenant," Pulliman nodded, staring at him impatiently.

Laybourne realized the man was waiting on the order to make the jump and so he gave it.

"Onward into the deeps," Laybourne said, faking a smile as he dreaded the nausea that was about to claw at his guts.

"Jump!" Pulliman barked at his crew.

The Cerebus shimmered as she blinked out of existence.

****

Two weeks earlier on Ventari VII

The night sky was filled with stars. They glowed hot and bright against the darkness above. Merb sat on top of the hill behind his house watching them. His whole life he had dreamed of leaving Ultan and exploring them. His father had been one of the cosmonauts the world government allowed to leave Ultan's surface during the construction of the planet's defense grid. No one remembered his father as they did Raken Pym or any of the pilots that were part of those missions. Merb's father was a part of Pym's crew though. He was the tech who dreamed up the orbital defense platforms that now protected Ultan from otherworldly threats. A race who called themselves the Kep'at had visited Ultan many cycles ago when his father had been but a boy himself. At first they seemed so wondrous, saviors come from the stars to deliver the world of Ultan. Their true colors became apparent within a matter of days. It had taken years though to drive the Kep'at from Ultan. Even then, there was no true victory against the vile aliens. The Kep'at were not truly defeated. They were only shown how costly it would be for them to remain on Ultan. The streets had run red with the blood Ultanians who gave their lives to make the Kep'at leave. In the wake of that disastrous war, all Ultanians were left with the knowledge of two things; they were not alone in the universe and their world was vulnerable to another such incursion should the Kep'at or another race like them return.

The Ultanian world government created the S.D.C. or Space Defense Coalition. Its primary purpose and directive was to develop a means to defend Ultan against such future encounters with alien life. As part of this directive, the S.D.C. also worked on creating space travel so that those of the Ultanian race could also touch the stars. Merb's father was one of those early dreamers and an extremely gifted engineer.

The S.D.C.'s goals were ambitious, yes, but Kep'at tech on the planet, which had been abandoned during the days of the war, gave them an edge. Most of the Kep'at tech was simply too advanced to be reverse engineered but not all of it. In the span of twenty cycles, Ultanians went from being a race without star travel to one that could achieve limited travel to the other planets of their own star system.

There were those who feared the S.D.C.'s efforts would serve as nothing more than a signal to other races like the Kep'at, an invitation to come to Ultan and claim it as their own. The more fringe elements went so far as to claim that the S.D.C. had long known of the existence of alien life and had been actively trying to make contact with the beings that dwelt among the stars. Thankfully, such voices were in the minority and the S.D.C.'s work continued.

Merb remembered just how proud he had been of his father and how much he wanted to grow up to follow in his footsteps. His father died doing what he loved in service to his people. No one could ask for a more meaningful death than that. However, even his father had hinted to him in private that the S.D.C. kept knowledge locked away from the general populace. His father never told him anything directly or shared what Merb suspected were secrets about the Ultan race's past and origins.

His mother fell apart on the day the soldiers arrived on their doorsteps to deliver the news of his father's death. She never recovered either, not really. Merb knew she loved him and that her heart was in the right place, but she simply didn't understand how much his father and the stars meant to him. She had discouraged all his efforts towards becoming the man his father had been but there was no denying that Merb was gifted. In the end, the two of them had met one another halfway. Merb endured the courses on farming and business his mother pushed on him while he continued to study engineering and the basic principles of astrogation.

Yesterday had been the breaking point. His acceptance letter from the S.D.C. arrived while he was visiting with their neighbor's son and his lifelong friend, Shelley. Upon his return home, she met him at the door to their home and confronted him. Both of them said things that time would surely make them regret. Merb knew he already regretted much of what he screamed at her. With tears flowing along the curves of her cheeks, she locked herself in her bedroom while he fled to this hilltop where he and his father had spent so many nights during the time they were allowed by God to share.

Merb checked his chronometer. In just a few hours, the sun would begin to rise and would need to face his mother again as he went into the house to collect his things. He was due to report to the S.D.C.'s training facilities by noon.

He lifted his face towards the stars and drank in their distant light. Faith taught that God had created all life but science taught that life was not created here on Ultan but elsewhere. Everything the scientists and historians had supposedly cobbled together since the birth of civilization on Ultan pointed to a world called Earth as the origin point of the Ultanian race. Merb couldn't help but wonder if the people of Earth were like those here. Did they play games? Did they sleep and dream? Did they have families? How much of their culture had survived whatever occurred that stranded them here on Ultan all those cycles past?

Merb saw something flash in the sky, amid the stars. Whatever it was, it was there and then gone in an instant. He smiled, hoping that it was his father reaching out to him from Heaven, assuring him that he was doing the right thing by leaving his mother to join the ranks of the S.D.C.

****

Captain Jonas Fleck was the ranking officer on duty at the S.D.C. Space Watch Center. The reports he was getting chilled him to the bone as he stood behind the officer manning the center's primary sensor data console. *Something* had just entered the atmosphere around Ultan. Whatever it was, it was massive. Its entry flash had been seen all over this side of Ultan. The giant object had broken apart before the planet's defense grid could lock on and target it. Now its pieces fell like rain onto the unsuspecting populace he and his men were responsible for protecting.

"Defense fighters scrambling now, sir," Lieutenant Hudshaw informed him.

Captain Fleck knew none of the fighters would reach the objects descending towards the planet in time to engage them, but protocol was protocol and they had to try to do something.

The objects bore no resemblance to anything on record that the Kep'at had ever used during their invasion and occupation of Ultan. His emergency request to access the files left over from the Ultan's computer core had been approved, but there was nothing there in the records from Earth that gave him a clue as to what these things were either. He had to assume they were hostile, but at this point, he didn't even know if they were manned craft or merely pieces of some metallic asteroid that spontaneously blew up on contact with Ultan's atmosphere.

"We've got reports of the objects impacting the continent all across both seaboards," Hudshaw told him. "So far, none have struck any populated areas."

On all of Ultan, there was only one truly populated and civilized continent. There simply weren't enough of Ultanians to make use of all the space the planet had to offer. Perhaps, if the Kep'at hadn't attacked the planet, its population would be higher and Ultanian civilization would have spread further outwards across the world. As it stood, the entire planet's population was a mere two million. That was a lot more than the original hive-style, terraforming ship that crashed on it had carried, but even back then, that number was a small one.

The general populace of Ultan didn't have a clue that the name for their planet came from the name of the ship that had carried their ancestors here. Most didn't even know that they were truly humans. The S.D.C. went to great efforts to keep the real origins of life on Ultan and what its people were a secret known only to the S.D.C. and the highest levels of civilian government. Captain Fleck had heard stories over his years with the S.D.C. about folks who had tried to share the truth. They'd been promptly discredited, and more often than not, whisked away by S.D.C. soldiers, never to be seen again.

Admiral Vetar wasn't a tyrant. In fact, from what Captain Fleck knew of him, he was rather the opposite in all regards other than the knowledge of where the Ultanian race had truly came from. Higher officers Fleck had discussed the matter with shared this opinion. Their explanation was that Vetar and those who had led before him believed that knowledge of Earth and their inability to reach it would only serve to harm the residents of Ultan and cause discord. It was an easy-enough thing to believe and a subject no one with any brains in their skull pressed.

Captain Fleck tore himself out of his thoughts and forced himself to focus on the crisis at hand. "Both seaboards?" he asked. "Do you have a clear dispersal pattern for the falling fragments yet?"

"A rough one," Hudshaw nodded. "Every single piece of whatever that thing was seems to be landing on this continent or in the waters off its coasts."

"That doesn't make any sense," Captain Fleck argued. "They should be coming down every on Ultan. Are you reading any sign for powered drives?"

"No, sir," Hudshaw answered. "Not that we have the capacity to detect at any rate."

"From how that thing exploded up there, those pieces should be hitting everywhere across this hemisphere not just here."

"Yes, sir," Hudshaw agreed.

In the minutes that had passed, just like Captain Fleck had predicted, none of the intercept fighters had managed to make contact with the fragments in air. All of the pieces of the object had reached the surface without resistance. The fighters lacked the sensor capabilities that the S.D.C. Space Watch Center possessed. Their sensor abilities only extended to targeting systems, radar, and line-of-sight visuals. They were built for speed, battle, and not much else.

"Call back the fighters," Captain Fleck ordered. "They're useless now."

Fleck's head was throbbing from the stress he was under. He rubbed at his temples trying to make the pain stop. He lacked the authority to declare martial law until the objects could be dealt with. There was nothing else he could do with the resources he had at hand. It was time to call Admiral Vetar.

****

"Jump complete. All systems green," the *Cerebus*'s navigator reported to Captain Pulliman.

Laybourne stood next to the captain's command chair or rather leaned against it, trying not to be sick. His innards felt as if they were spinning, his guts twisted in a hundred different ways. He managed to hold himself together and keep at least a token shred of his dignity.

As the Cerebus moved through space to enter orbit around Ventari VII, Laybourne found he was already feeling better. No matter how brief the sickness brought on by a FTL jump might be, it was never brief enough.

Captain Pulliman appeared to be perfectly fine as Laybourne noticed the man looking at him with concern. "Are you okay, Lieutenant?"

"Allergic to jump meds," Laybourne grunted, letting go of the side of the captain's chair and standing on his own again. "I'm fine."

With a look of pity, Captain Pulliman turned his gaze from Laybourne. It fell on the image of Ventari VII which filled the Cerebus's forward view screen. "We're under cloak, Lieutenant, and moving into orbit now. There is no sign that we have been detected by the planet's inhabitants."

"Sir!" one of the bridge officers yelled at the captain, his eyes wide with shock. "There appears to be an orbital defense grid in place around Ventari VII!"

"What? That's impossible! Execute evasive maneuvers, pattern Delta 9," Pulliman raged and then turned his fury towards Laybourne as the Cerebus rolled in space, shifting the course of her approach to Ventari VII. "You said the population of this world wasn't capable of space travel!"

"It's been over twenty years since the last time the Alliance sent a probe this far out according to the reports Colonel Hell gave me. A lot can change in two decades," Laybourne told Pulliman, trying to keep his tone calm despite the captain's anger being directed at him.

Pulliman snapped around, demanding more information about the defense grid from his crew.

"It's a rudimentary satellite grid sir," one of the ship's sensor techs told him. "If it had detected us already, we'd know it. The satellites are all armed with low-grade missiles. I doubt if even a concentrated barrage from the grid could even do any real damage to our shields."

"That's not the point," Laybourne said hurriedly, taking control of the situation. "We need to make sure we're not detected."

Captain Pulliman glared at him. "This is my ship, Lieutenant. It is best you keep that in mind no matter how much authority the colonel has given you. If those satellites pose a danger to her, you can bet I will blow them out of the sky."

"Your sensor tech over there just told you those things are so old fashioned they can't hurt this ship and you know it's true. Now get us past them and onto the surface before those satellites do figure out we're here," Laybourne ordered.

"Sirs," the sensor tech, whose name badge read Carlson, interrupted them. "I am picking up some crazy readings from the planet. The entire population seems to have been centered on one continent."

"That's not too strange if it's a colony world we're dealing with," Pulliman commented.

"Wait," Laybourne barked. "What do you mean by 'have been'?

"The readings I am getting show large industrialized, urban cities all across the continent, sir. Far too large for the amount of life signs I'm picking up for them to be occupied." Carlson paused, double checking his data. "The life signs my instruments are reading clearly appear human in nature. I'm getting some other odd readings though that I can't identify. Those are the more numerous of the two."

"The Kep'at's new allies are already here," Laybourne muttered.

"We have no reason to believe that, Lieutenant," Captain Pulliman ordered. "There are no signs of recent FTL transits or enemy vessels for that matter. Whatever has happened down there was more likely a planetary event. We've all heard of civilizations that have wiped themselves out before through war, bio-engineering gone wrong; planetary disasters come in many forms."

"I'm not buying that, Captain," Laybourne scowled at Pulliman. "Our intel says this world is slated to be the Kep'at new allies' first target and we show up to find its residents nearly wiped out. I'd say that's one heck of coincidence, wouldn't you?"

"The defense grid around Ventari VII is still intact, Laybourne," Pulliman pointed out. "That too points to a planetary event. I mean, it's clear they had the tech to at least try to put up a fight if this new race jumped in. Don't you think they would have when they saw them coming? Kep'at ships don't have the cloaking tech that we do."

"That defense grid is junk by our standards, right?" Laybourne asked, looking to Carlson for support.

"Yes, sir," Carlson nodded. "Not only has it still failed to detect us, but the closer scans we've taken of it suggest that entire sections of it are offline but not damaged. It's more as if they were shut down from the surface and never reactivated."

Pulliman appeared relieved.

Laybourne was too. Their mission depended heavily on stealth until they were ready to make contact with Ventari VII's populace on their terms. Whatever had happened down there though had been *bad* and he had even less of an idea what they would be facing when they landed now.

"We stick to the colonel's plan," Laybourne told Pulliman. "You get us down there and my ground pounders will take it from there. Just put us down somewhere rural like I said but not so far out that reaching one of those cities is going to be a nightmare."

Pulliman nodded and turned to his bridge crew, barking orders.

****

Two weeks earlier on Ventari VII

After seeing the flash in the sky, Merb had opted to call it a night and head back home despite the chance of waking up his mother. He had snuck into the house through the window of his bedroom. He still couldn't sleep though. He didn't know if it was the stress of dealing with his mother's hatred for the S.D.C. or the excitement of reporting to join it at dawn. It was very late and he knew he should try to sleep some. The stories he heard about S.D.C. boot were the stuff of nightmares and he was going to need all the energy he could get. None the less, instead of sliding under the covers of his bed, he plopped himself down at his desk and booted up his net connection hoping to find news about what the flash in the sky he had seen was. There was nothing in the news about the flash though, at least not directly. The S.D.C. had however issued a warning to all citizens to stay in their homes until further notice. The warning was an odd one and Merb wondered if the two things were related.

At first, he wondered if the Kep'at had returned, but there was no sign of that. If they had, surely the entire night sky would be lit up even now by the Ultan Defense Grid engaging their forces. No, it was more likely the flash he saw was some kind of meteor that made contact with Ultan's upper atmosphere and had broken up as it came down.

Merb scanned through numerous more news broadcasts and bulletins but couldn't find anything more than the warning. It was being broadcast everywhere and that was scary.

He had studied long and hard to join the S.D.C. so he knew a lot more about things like this than most folks and the warning worried him. There were no reports of whatever he had seen coming down either and he knew it had to have done so by now. The dispersal pattern for an object large enough to cause a flash like the one he saw surely would have put some of the thing's fragments striking the populated portions of the continent.

Frustrated, he started doing his own math, supposing that the flash he saw had indeed been something that broke up in Ultan's atmosphere. He could only guess at its real mass of course but tried to keep his numbers as realistic as he could. After a few minutes, he stared at his computer's screen in disbelief. If his numbers were anywhere close to right, a piece of the thing he saw should have come down in the next valley over. He hadn't heard an explosion though and surely such an event would have caused a huge one that shook the ground for miles.

Outside, he heard the engines of military fighters howling through the night sky. They were T-18s. He could tell. He had always wanted to fly one. They were built to intercept and engage inner atmospheric threats to Ultan.

Merb raced to his window hoping to catch a glance of them, but they were gone by the time he reached it.

As his gaze fell from looking upwards at the sky, out towards the valley his projections had put the object coming down in, he saw *something* he had never imagined possible. There was darkness, darker than the night around it, emanating from the area where the object would have struck. It seemed to eat what little light there was in the night in the direction of the valley.

Merb turned off the light in his bedroom and stained his eyes, trying to see into the darkness as best he could. There appeared to be things moving within it. He couldn't make out the exact shapes of the creatures but they were roughly the size of a full grown man . . . and they were coming out of the valley in waves. Something deep down told him he needed to run.

All Merb could think about was saving his mother as he slung open the door to his closet and dug around for the rifle his father had given him for hunting when he was younger. He found it, snatching it up into his trembling hands. He fumbled with the weapon, checking to see if it was loaded. It wasn't. With a curse, he sat it beside the closest door and got down on his hands knees, searching the closest floor for the box of bullets he kept there buried among his clothes and mounds of outgrown toys from years gone by.

He tossed toys and clothes all over his room as he dug madly trying to find the box of ammo. When he finally did, it took him another full two minutes to crams a few rounds into his rifle. Only then did he risk returning to the window to see what was happening in the darkness outside.

****

The *Cerebus*'s landing engines spat flame that scorched the ground beneath her as she sat down on Ventari VII. First Lieutenant Laybourne didn't tarry on her bridge. He knew Captain Pulliman and his crew had things well under control and he had already given orders to keep the ship cloaked.

They sat down about twenty miles from the closest city. The area Laybourne picked was a rural one and mostly woodlands below the massive hill that the *Cerebus* now rested upon. According to the orbital scans, there were several small clusters of scattered dwelling between here and the city. Laybourne wanted to check those out first before he dove head on into making full-out contact with the planet's population. Assuming there was still a civilization left to make contact with and not just the remnants of one as those same scans suggested.

Laybourne headed to Hangar Bay 1 where his own men were waiting on him. Colonel Hell had given him command of nearly a tenth of the Hell's Banshees overall fighting strength. He didn't need that kind of firepower right now. Stealth remained the key to how he wanted to approach things until he had a clearer picture of what he was dealing with on Ventari VII. To that end, he had Sergeant Robinson assemble a platoon of two dozen men who would be accompanying him off the *Cerebus*.

Sergeant Robinson and the platoon saluted as he approached them. The rest of the hangar bay was utter chaos as the squad of Mech and tank crews worked hurriedly to get ready in case they were needed sooner than expected.

Laybourne cast a longing gaze at one of the mech suits that sat nearby. It stood roughly ten feet tall. Its armor was painted in the green and yellow colors of the Banshees. Its left hand was a giant - sized imitation of a human one, complete with five fingers and thumb. The end of its right arm was massive, tri-barrel cannon. The missile launcher units that rested within each of its shoulders were extended and open for loading. Laybourne had a passion for mechs. He'd been in enough fights with the suits at his side to know just how tough the things were. Nothing short of a state of the art tank stood a chance against them on the ground. These new Mark IXs were supposed to be even faster and more maneuverable than the ones he had shared the battlefield with on Dennab II. An appreciative whistle escaped his lips.

"Those things are nice, sir," Sergeant Robinson said with a smirk, "but they're death traps too."

Laybourne could only nod in agreement. If you were the enemy and you saw mechs like these coming across the battlefield at you, you could dang well bet they'd be the target of the fire you could throw at them. Mechs were tough, but they weren't tanks. They simply couldn't haul around the amount of armor a tank could and still function as they were designed to. They had more weak spots and it was easier to land a "lucky" shot on them. What he supposed Robinson meant though was that if you were piloting a mech, there was no way to bail like there was with a tank. If the inside of your suit caught on fire, you got roasted along with all the electronics around, cooked inside a metal tomb. And just as bad, if you're power supply gave out or your motors locked, you were stranded and a sitting duck with no means of escape until the battle was over and someone arrived to help you out of the suit. Even so, the speed and firepower of a mech suit was enough to make Laybourne wish sometimes that he had been assigned to a mech unit instead of infantry when he joined the Banshees.

"Are the men ready?" Laybourne asked Robinson.

"As they'll ever be, sir," Robinson replied with a shrug. "A lot of them are unbloodied newbies."

Laybourne chuckled. "We were too once and we're still here."

Robinson grunted in response before Laybourne stepped up in front of the assembled to platoon to address it.

"At this time, this op is not considered a combat one. Do not fire at any target unless fired upon or you are ordered to do so," Laybourne's voice boomed. "Our objective is merely to get a feel of what's out there. We know very little about this planet and less about its inhabitants. The plan is to make contact, not go in guns blazing. Do I make myself clear?"

The voices of the platoon answered as one, "Yes, sir!"

Laybourne scanned the ranks of the soldiers and was glad to see T'chal and Leon among them. He knew he could count on them to help keep the newbies alive in things went all pear-shaped out there. The two of them were also the only non-human members of the platoon. That was good too as the platoon's medic barely looked old enough to shave. All Banshee medics were supposed to be trained to deal with the basic first aid needs of any lifeform they encountered, but Laybourne knew from experience that very few of them were. It wasn't anyone's fault. There were just so many races in the Banshees and in the known section of space that it was all just too much to learn for most of them. Medics weren't doctors. They were essentially paramedics with limited training and often only a short time to learn it in.

The young medic's name badge on his uniform read Johnny. He was burly and compact with a wide forehead above overly thick eyebrows. His short cropped brown hair was curly and only added to his youthful appearance.

Laybourne stepped up to him. "How old are you Banshee?"

"Eighteen, sir!" the young medic barked at him.

"And how did you end up in *my* platoon?"

"Top of my class, sir!"

"How many drops?"

"Counting this one, sir?"

Laybourne nodded slowly.

"One, sir!"

Laybourne frowned.

The young medic saw his frown and added, "I'll do the colonel proud, sir!"

"See that you do," Laybourne ordered and continued inspecting the rest of the platoon.

When he finished, he returned to his spot beside Sergeant Robinson.

"We'll be approaching the closest city through the woodlands just to the south of it. Again, I caution you be prepared for anything but also to hold your fire unless you are given orders otherwise."

With that, Laybourne nodded to Sergeant Robinson. Robinson nodded back at him.

"Fall out!" Robinson ordered the platoon. "Leon, you have point!"

Laybourne fell in with the center of the platoon as the soldiers headed towards and then down the landing ramp out of the *Cerebus*'s hangar area.

****

Ventari VII was so Earth-like it almost gave Laybourne the creeps. The woods the platoon marched through were lush and green. The branches of the wood's tall trees shielded the platoon from the most of the midday sun. The temperature and humidity was very much that of summertime on Earth.

Though the vegetation was beautiful and clearly thriving, there were no signs of animal life. That struck Laybourne as odd. Any world like this one should have been teeming with wildlife; but there simply was nothing, at least that he could see, hear, or smell, in the woods with them.

Suddenly, Leon stopped and held up a hand indicating for the rest of the platoon to do the same.

Laybourne clutched his rifle tighter, holding it ready. He'd known Leon long enough to know that the alien soldier wasn't prone to doing things without a good reason. If he'd called for a stop, the platoon might be in serious danger.

Leon motioned for Laybourne to join him at the front of the column. He moved to do so, moving as quietly as he could.

"Something's not right here, sir," Leon whispered.

"What?" Laybourne asked, scanning the trees around them in search of whatever had caused Leon to halt the platoon.

"There's nothing here, sir," Leon said. "This place should be crawling with wild game."

Leon twisted his head to look into Laybourne's eyes. "There aren't even any birds here, sir."

"The radiological and biological threat detectors are reading green," Laybourne said glancing at the small capsule-shaped device pinned to the breast of his combat vest.

Leon nodded. "I know. That's part of what worries me. It's like something simply scared everything here away."

"Well, we can't just stop here," Laybourne pointed out. "We have to keep moving."

"There's a clearing up ahead and a dwelling of some sort in it," Leon told him. "I suggest we head there.

"Agreed." Laybourne kept his new place at the front of the column with Leon as the platoon started moving again.

The woods ended, opening into a wide clearing with hills and valleys that stretched as far as even Leon's hawk-like vision could see on its other side. Within in the clearing was a lone house. It looked like something one might see in history videos of Earth. It appeared to be mainly built of wood and covered over with a light alloy siding. The siding was scratched and torn away from the house in numerous areas. Its front door lay in pieces, as if something big and strong had just charged through it.

Laybourne ordered the platoon to hold. "Leon, get in there and check the place out."

Leon shot him an angry glare but then shrugged and headed into the house. He emerged a few minutes later, carrying a primitive hunting rifle. Leon tossed it at Laybourne's feet.

"There was a fight of some kind in the house, sir," Leon told him. "I found two human bodies, badly mangled."

"Human?" Laybourne asked, his eyes going wide.

"Yes, sir," Leon nodded. "Red-blooded humans. Their blood was all over the place."

"That's not all I found though, sir," Leon continued. "The other body, well, you really need to see it for yourself, sir."

Laybourne followed Leon into the house. The area that must have been its living room was trashed. A table lay broken near an overturned couch. A shattered lamp left shards of glass covering the floor. The glass crunched under Laybourne's heavy combat boots as he followed Leon towards a set of stairs leading up to the house's second floor. As they neared the stairs, there were shell casings everywhere. It was clear they came from the rifle Leon had carried out of the house. The body of a young man, or rather part of it, rested on the stairs. The young man had been ripped in half. The lower half of his body was nowhere to be seen. The top half of the young man's body leaked strands of bloated, purple intestines which sprawled over the stairs like the corpses of snakes.

"Kid sure put up a fight," Leon commented. "He got one of the things coming after him too."

Leon pointed towards the other side of the living room. Just in front of the doorway that looked to lead to the house's kitchen lay another body. It was human in shape but the resemblance ended there. The purple flesh of its naked form was riddled with bullet holes. Whatever it was, it had two arms and two legs but its entire upper half was also covered in tentacles that grew out of its body. They were limp and rotting now, but Laybourne could see clearly that they had been strong and deadly when the creature had been alive.

A pool of yellowish blood had formed on the floor around the creature and dried there. The smell of it was like brine mixed with urine. Laybourne nearly gagged as its odor hit him.

"Whatever that thing is, sir," Leon said, "I've never seen or heard of anything like it."

Laybourne let those words sink in. Both of them had seen a lot of strange crap with the Banshees, but Leon had been a bounty hunter before he joined up. At least that's what he claimed to have been. Laybourne suspected his work must have been closer to that of an assassin's. Leon had been to more star systems than Laybourne was likely to see in his whole life and not just because the average age of a Banshee was below fifty standard years.

"I don't think whatever that thing is native to Ventari VII," Leon said.

The scene before him was a lot to take in. Humans weren't supposed to be here. This world was supposed to be off limits to the Alliance due to its proximity to Kep'at space. Beyond that, the creature wasn't armed. Heck, it wasn't even clothed. It looked like some kind of primitive predator out of a primal nightmare.

"There's another dead human upstairs," Leon pointed at the ceiling. "Female and older. Could be she was this kid's mother and that was why he put up such a fight down here."

"Makes sense," Laybourne agreed. "But that doesn't tell us anything about where that monster came from or what it was doing here. For that matter, what the devil are humans doing here?"

Leon shrugged. "You're the CO. You figure it out. My job is just to point the way and kill things remember?"

Laybourne laughed despite the grizzly scene around them.

"You wanna go up and take a look at the old lady?"

"Do I need to?"

Leon shook his head. "I don't suppose so, sir. She's as messed as this kid. Both of them look to have been eaten on too."

Laybourne took a closer look at the kid's corpse. He saw it now. The missing chunks of flesh as if teeth had dug into the kid and ripped them off.

"So much for making contact with the natives." Laybourne sighed. He had hoped there would be someone alive in the house, someone they could question and get a better picture of what Ventari VII had in store for them.

Sergeant Robinson's voice boomed over the comm piece of Laybourne's helmet. "LT! We've got movement!"

Laybourne could see that Leon had heard Robinson too. Leon's heightened senses were sometimes scary.

Both of them rushed out of the house. The platoon had spread out in a defensive formation around the house, guns facing the woods they'd emerged from earlier.

Laybourne fell in beside Robinson. "Report!" he ordered.

"There's something out there, sir," Robinson said. "Nobody's got a visual on it yet but it's there. I'd stake my life on it."

A tree swayed as if something had bumped against it. One of the newbies in the platoon lost his cool and opened up in the direction of the movement. High-velocity rounds splintered woods as the newbie sprayed the trees on full auto fire.

"Hold fire! Hold fire!" Laybourne yelled.

Another Banshee beside the panicking newbie had to slam the kid in the back between his shoulders to get the kid to let up. The older soldier took the kid's rifle out of his hands.

Everything went eerily silent.

Laybourne held his rifle ready, still watching the trees. "Leon?"

"I don't see anything out there sir," Leon answered.

"Okay, let's—" Laybourne started but then all Hell broke loose.

The very ground itself in front of the platoon heaved and vomited up monsters. The things came tearing their way out of the dirt. They were just like the dead creature inside the house only very much alive and ready to make sure Laybourne's men never left this place alive.

As one, the soldiers of the platoon reacted. Guns chattered, spewing shell casings, as bullets raked the ranks of the monsters but the things were already in hand-to-hand combat range. Tentacles whipped through the air like slashing blades.

Laybourne saw one Banshee take a blow that sliced his both his helmet and his skull open. Brain matter and bone fragments flew from the wound as the man toppled over.

The creatures fought with their tentacles and hands, overpowering a good number of Banshees in the platoon before they got off more than a few bursts. Laybourne could see that they were all going to die unless he did something fast.

"Fallback!" Laybourne shouted. "Into the house!"

The few Banshees, who weren't already in the clutches of the monsters from the dirt that could, made for the house's open doorway. Laybourne hoped the things couldn't come through the house's floor. If the scene he'd seen inside it was any indication, they couldn't.

Leon had slung his rifle onto his shoulder and was fighting with his twin energy knives. One of the creatures lay dead near him. Its face was a mangled mass of cut-up tissue. A second one of the creatures was striking at Leon again and again with its lashing tentacles, but Leon met each attack with slashing blade that burnt its way through the tentacles' thick muscles.

Laybourne jerked his rifle to his shoulder and aimed at the thing Leon was engaged with. He put a burst of rounds in its back. The creature shrieked, its tentacles flailing skyward in pain and surprise. Leon took advantage of the opening Laybourne's burst gave him. He rushed in on the creature and cut its throat from one side to the other. The creature slumped forward, falling to the ground, as Leon sprang away from it.

"Into the house!" Laybourne screamed at him.

Leon's long legs pumped as he sprinted for the doorway, meeting Laybourne there. Laybourne clicked his rifle up to full auto and hosed the creatures closing on them as Leon darted on inside.

The surviving members of the platoon had spread out in the house's living room, all the barrels of their weapons pointed at the doorway as Laybourne dove inside and to its right. As soon as he was clear from their line of fire, the Banshees poured fire through the doorway at the monsters outside the house.

The battle ended as quickly as it had started. The creatures borrowed their way into the ground with impossible speed and were gone from sight in an instant.

"What the hell were those things?" a young Banshee soldier Laybourne thought went by the name of Hardtower screamed.

Sergeant Robinson was already barking orders to the platoon's survivors as Laybourne got to his feet.

"I want this place secured!" Robinson shouted as Laybourne looked over at Leon.

Leon was covered in the yellow goo that passed from the creature's blood. He had shut down the blades of his knives and sheathed them, holding his rifle in his hands again.

"Those things were blasted fast, sir," Leon commented. "I mean even by my standards."

Five minutes passed like hours as the platoon secured the house as best they could and Laybourne took count of who was left alive. The count was a hell of a lot lower than he would have liked. He'd left the *Cerebus* with thirty men. Now, he had twelve. The monsters had hit them fast, hard, and caught them completely off guard. His Banshees had paid the price for it too. Laybourne tried not to blame himself. There was no way anyone could have guessed things like those monsters would be in the bloody dirt of Ventari VII, waiting on them.

He spotted Johnny patching up a Banshee who had sustained several long gashes to his arms and exposed face from one of the monsters' tentacles. The young medic appeared to holding up better than Laybourne thought he would and looked to be bloody dang good at his job too.

Laybourne waited on Johnny to finish with the soldier he was working on then called Johnny to him.

"I know what you're going to ask, sir," Johnny said before Laybourne could even get the question out. "And the answer is, I don't know."

"That's not good enough," Laybourne faked a growl, trying to intimidate the young medic.

"Sir, I'm just a combat medic. I don't have the training or the equipment to tell you if those things carry anything we need to worry about at this point," Johnny said calmly. "I wouldn't rule it out though. The infection in the wounds on the two men I have treated so far appears to be spreading faster than it should. There's no sign of any outright poisoning though, and that's a good thing."

Laybourne grunted. "Keep me informed," he ordered.

Johnny nodded and moved onto his next patient.

In all, five of the dozen surviving members of the platoon had taken wounds from the creatures. Only one of them was hurt too bad to carry on. T'chal had returned the living room's couch to its normal position and laid the wounded Banshee on it. The woman's name was Barta. Laybourne had been with her on drops before and knew she was one tough lady. Now though, she sprawled on the couch with sweat dripping from her hair and a feverish, spaced-out hollowness to her eyes. Her right arm was dislocated from her shoulder and its length was covered with bite marks from the tiny mouths that lined the underside of the monsters' tentacles.

Sergeant Robinson and Leon came up to Laybourne where he stood staring at Barta.

"Just how fragged are we, sir?" Robinson demanded to know.

Laybourne shook his head. "We should be okay, I think, in here. Those things don't seem to be able to come up through the floor."

"They can sure come through the doors and windows though," Leon pointed out, gesturing at the body of the rotting creature T'chal had moved from the house's kitchen doorway to the corner of the room.

Laybourne nodded. "Yeah, but we can see them coming then. They don't appear to be armed."

"Other than those tentacles," Leon reminded him.

"Other than tooth and nail kind of stuff, yeah. Our guns give us the advantage as long as we can see them coming," Laybourne popped the mag from his rifle and slammed a fresh one into it.

"We should call the *Cerebus* from some back up and get the hell out of here while we still can," Robinson spat on the floor then wiped the corner of his mouth with the backside of his hand.

"No," Laybourne said, leaving no room for argument. "We need to find out what these things are and where they come from."

"Are you thinking they're these new allies of the Kep'at the brass keeps talking about?" Leon asked.

"We can't rule that out," Laybourne shrugged.

"Those things sure don't look like they're even capable of rational thought much less flying a starship to this world to conquer it," Robinson said, pointing at the corpse of the monster in the corner. "Take a look at that thing. I mean a real good look. Those things aren't much more than animals."

"You've been a Banshee long enough to know that you can't judge things by their appearance, Robinson. Doing that can get you killed real quick," Laybourne told the sergeant and then turned to Leon. "What do you think?"

"Like I said, it's not my job to think," Leon answered and walked away from Laybourne. "Let me know when you need me to kill something again."

Laybourne gritted his teeth in frustration.

"I really suggest we make contact with the ship, sir," Robinson urged him again.

"Fine," Laybourne relented. "Have the *Cerebus* roll out our tanks and get the mechs down here too. You're right. We can't just sit in this house and do nothing. We need to press on towards the city and find out what in the hell is going down on this whacked out planet."

****

Corporal Robert Nash was in command of Blackwing squad. It was comprised of his own Mark XI mech and three more of the powerful killing machines. The servo-motors of his whined as Nash poured more power into them and his mech bounded through the trees. *Through the trees.* The Mark XIs were armored up and strong enough to pay the trees in their path little mind.

The LT's platoon was holed up in a house on the far side of these woods and Nash was determined to reach them ASAP. His mechs had been ready when the call for reinforcements came. The company's tanks were still gearing up. They'd roll out too as soon as they were ready, but Nash knew it was up to him and his Blackwings to reach the LT right now.

Each Blackwing was capable of a peak speed of thirty miles an hour and he was pushing his squad close to that max. It was a gamble as they had some distance to cover and maintaining such speed for any prolonged period risked the mechs' motors in their legs burning out. Blackwings weren't built for speed but for firepower.

Captain Pulliman had briefed him and his squad personally on the LT's situation. It didn't sound the LT was really in over his head, yet, but Nash knew things could change in a heartbeat and didn't plan on leaving the LT in the wind.

The creatures that had the LT trapped were apparently subterranean in nature. They swam through the ground like a fish would the water from how Pulliman told him the LT had described them. The creatures weren't armed with anything other than tentacles and claws. That part was good at least. It meant he didn't have to worry about some sniper locking onto his butt with a shoulder rocket.

The Blackwings' sensors were top of the line but they weren't designed to track things that traveled in the ground and as powerful as their weapons were, Nash doubted they could do any serious damage to the creatures plaguing the LT unless the things came topside and exposed themselves to the Blackwings' fire.

Nash had taken point himself in his headlong rush to reach the LT's position. He didn't notice the pit ahead of him until his Blackwing was careening into it. The pit was partly camouflaged by the darkness that had fallen as Ventari VII's sun had set and partly by the density of the woods. Nash cursed himself for not being more alert and plowing into it though. It was a rookie mistake.

He loosed a litany of curses as his Blackwing crashed into the far side of the pit and bounced backwards against its other side like ping pong ball bouncing between paddles. He felt the impacts as they jarred him inside the mech. Emergency lights were going off all over the tactical display on the panel in front his face. He managed to scream a warning that stopped the others of his squad from tumbling into the pit as well. According to his display, they came to stop just short of the pit's edge and now waited to see what his condition was.

It wasn't good. The fall and impact had done a great deal of damage to his mech's legs. Its own weight causing to the servo-motors in them to short out and break as they met the rock bottom of the pit. All the mech's other systems were functional though. He still had weapons and enough use of the mech's arms to use them to heave the large suit out of the pit. Nash, using only the suit's arms as that was all he had left to move with, piloted the Blackwing up and out of the pit.

When he stopped, the mech lay beside the pit's edge, its legs not much more than crumpled and bent metal under its torso.

He was about to demand a sit-rep from his men when the creatures showed themselves. They came from everywhere around the squad, lunging up from beneath the ground at them. The mechs were surrounded by the enemy before they could even respond. That didn't stop them from responding though. The heavy, right hand cannon tri-barrels of the mechs spun spraying death into the creatures. Many of the creatures were almost disintegrated by the sweeping arcs of point blank that slammed into them. One creature's upper body became a mess of exploding chunks of flesh and red mist that lingered in the air where it had once been.

Nash jumped out of instinctual fear as his display screen was filled with a close up shot of one of the creatures as it used its two human like hands to grab onto the front of the armored head of his mech. Its tentacles thudded like pounding flails. Each impact dented the mech's armor, scraping away its paint. Nash's display flickered from the beating and he heard crackling in the circuits that lined the inside of the suit around him. He lashed out with his mech's left hand, taking hold of one of the creature's legs. The bones there crunched from the pressure of the metal hand's grip. The creature shrieked in pain, trying to pull free. All of its tentacles whipped around pummeling the wrist of the hand that held it. Nash wouldn't have believed it possible for a biologic to do as much as the creature was to his mech. It was happening though. Sparks flew with each blow the tentacles landed on the wrist of his suit's left hand. Its servo-motors blew out. The mech's left hand still clutched the creature by the thing's broken leg but was otherwise useless.

Nash brought his mech's right hand around to bash in the creature's skull with a single, powerful blow. The creature flopped to the dirt, dead. Two more of the monsters came bounding towards his crippled mech where it lay at the edge of the pit.

Servo-motors whined as Nash raised the mech's right-handed tri-barrel at them. The tri-barrel spun. A blast of high-velocity, armor-piercing rounds met the two monsters head on. One of them died instantly taking the brunt of the blast. Its chest was pulped, spraying yellow blood, as the force of the blast sent it flying backwards. The second monster lost its right arm and leg to the blast as the heavy rounds ripped at that side of its body.

There was no time to check on the other members of his squad because still more of the monsters sprang onto Nash's crippled mech. He heard the thud of one of the things landing on the back of his mech. It set into him with its tentacles. Instead of using them like whips though, this monster somehow made its tentacles rigid. They stabbed into the back of his mech like spears. Half a dozen or more strikes from the tentacle spears rained down on him every second. Alarm klaxons were blaring in his ears. His mech's primary cooling system had failed and the monster on his back and was getting dangerously close to penetrating the mech's armor enough to strike at him inside it.

Nash rolled his mech, using most of the suit's remaining available power. The creature that was on his back was either caught too off guard or too stupid not to give up its position. It was caught underneath his mech and crushed into a wet stain on the ground beneath it. Still shooting, upside down, Nash managed to take out another of the monsters on its way towards him. Its legs were cut out from under it by the stream of fire from his tri-barrel. The upper part of its body hit the ground, still sliding towards him, carried on by its momentum. Before it died, one of its tentacles lashed outward, plunging into the face of his mech. Its tipped end penetrated the armor of Nash's mech and came bursting through the display screen before his eyes. It stopped less than inch from skewering him between his eyes.

Fires began to spring to life inside his suit. Nash could feel the heat of them burning his jumpsuit and his flesh beneath it. He screamed from the pain, his thumb depressing the emergency eject feature of his suit. The chest of the mech he was in exploded outward, decapitating an unlucky monster that had been closing in on him. It did Nash little good though. He was stuck inside the mech even though he'd blown open its chest. The mech's internal impact harness held him in place. Nash clawed at it as he smelt the meat of his own body being cooked by the fires that now fully raged inside his mech. He tried his comm, desperately attempting to call to for help only to find it completely offline.

One of the monsters leaped on top of his mech. He could feel its cold flesh touching him through the martial of his jumpsuit in the moment before three of the creature's tentacles plunged downwards, impaling him. Blood rose up his throat and came out of his mouth like erupting vomit. Nash struggled to breathe and found he couldn't. All he could do was writhe about inside the harness that held him as the creature twisted the tentacles piercing his body around inside of it.

Private Gary Sieger could see that Corporal Nash was dead. The corporal's damaged mech had been swarmed by the monsters that had sprang forth from the ground. The things covered the corporal's mech entirely now so thickly that hid it from view. Private Ferguson's mech was down too. In his panic, Private Intiga had hit Ferguson's mech, full on, with a sustained burst from his tri-barrel. At that short of range, such a burst did a lot more damage than even a Blackwing's armor could withstand. Ferguson's mech was little more than a pile of scrap metal.

He'd lost sight of Intiga as the newbie had made a run for it after mowing down Ferguson. The last he had seen of Intiga in Blackwing III was the newbie's rear side as his mech sprinted at max power into the trees.

Intiga could burn in Hell for all Sieger cared. All that mattered to Sieger right now was getting the frag out of the madness surrounding him alive. Bodies of the tentacle-covered monsters were scattered everywhere. He'd lost track of how many of the monsters he had taken out. Even so, if his suit's sensors were to be believed, he remained outnumbered two dozen to one. Those odds sucked but it was the hand he had been dealt, and Sieger wasn't giving up without a fight.

Sieger used his mech's human-like left hand to take hold of one of the creatures that had attached itself to his back and tear the thing loose. He pounded the monster into the ground over and over again until almost every bone in the thing's body surely had to be shattered. Even as he was doing so, he brought his mech's right hand around in a wide arc, hosing the other monsters closest to him on full auto. Their bodies spasmed and danced as heavy rounds ripped through them, leaving massive holes that leaked yellow blood in their wake. He knew it was "do or die" time as he flung the battered body of the creature his mech's left hand still clutched into another of its kind that came racing at him.

His mech stood up to its full height, tall and proud, as three of the monsters closed in enough to encircle it. Their tentacles stabbed at its armor, sometimes causing nothing more than sparks and scraped paint as they skidded harmlessly off. The blows that did damage though did a great deal of it. One of the tentacles landed a lucky strike that severed the ammo feed to Sieger's tri-barrel. Another slammed into the backside of his mech's right knee, causing it to give out. Sieger's mech dropped to onto one leg as used its tri-barrel hand as a club, caving in one of the creature's chests. The creature's ribs folded inward as blood came gushing up to erupt in a shower of yellow from its open mouth.

The blow to his mech's knee, thank God, hadn't damaged it beyond the point of being able to function. Sieger pushed his suit to its limits as it jumped up and pounced forward like the nuclear-powered juggernaut that it was. His mech steamrolled a path through the creatures that blocked its way, lumbering onwards toward the trees. Sieger's desperate attempt at escape was cut short as one of the monsters hurled itself onto the back of his mech and two of the thing's tentacles rammed downwards into the mech's power core. Sieger didn't even have time to curse as his mech's power core melted down and the woods blossomed into a fiery mass of nuclear fire.

****

Laybourne watched the fiery blast in the distance reaching skyward through the house's upstairs bedroom window.

"What was that?" T'chal rasped from where he stood beside Laybourne.

"It looked like some kind of mini nuclear detonation," Robinson said over Laybourne's shoulder.

Laybourne sighed. "That was likely our reinforcements."

Leon and Hardtower shared the bedroom with them. All of the remaining Banshees' of Laybourne's platoon had moved onto the house's second floor except for Johnny, who refused to leave the wounded Barta alone downstairs, and a Banshee named Preston who stayed to watch over them. Laybourne suspected that Preston had a *thing* with Barta. The man was as glued to her as Johnny was to his duty. Laybourne knew the three of them were in a very exposed position compared to the Banshees who had moved upstairs with him. The infection in Barta's wounds had continued to grow worse with each passing minute though, and she really couldn't be moved. He figured he could have ordered Johnny and Preston to leave her behind but that didn't seem right and he wasn't about to chance giving an order that wouldn't be carried out. Tensions were running high enough without the added conflict. Everyone knew this was his first command on this level and he wasn't about to do anything to make it more shaky than it already was.

No one had outright blamed him for the mess they were in, but he'd served under his share of newbie officers too in his day. He knew what had to be going through the minds of his men.

"What do you mean that was our reinforcements?" Robinson growled. "Corporal Nash was his way here with an entire squad of Blackwing Mechs. Ain't no way those monsters out there could have stopped them."

Laybourne shook his head. "You saw that blast same as I did. You wanna tell me what else we've seen on this planet that could create a blast like that one other than a mech's power core rupturing?"

Robinson's smashed a fist into the wall next to the window and Laybourne could see that the sergeant knew he was right. That didn't mean he liked it though.

Leon snickered where he stood near the bedroom door.

"What?" Laybourne asked, turning to the alien.

"Sir?" Leon grinned at him.

"Why did you do that?" Laybourne demanded.

"I was just thinking, sir," Leon told him. "If those things can take down a squad of mechs, I don't see why the floor of this house is stopping them from getting at us."

Laybourne felt himself going pale. "Frag me," Laybourne muttered. "You're right."

"So one has to wonder why those things are holding back then instead of just finishing us here and now." Leon's grin grew even wider along the lines of his angular features.

"I told you staying here was a bad idea," Robinson started in but Laybourne interrupted him.

"Stow it, Sergeant," Laybourne snapped. "We do need to move, though, and fast."

"Returning to the *Cerebus* would be the smartest move," Leon cut in. "Let's assume these things are indeed the Kep'at's new allies or rather expendable shock troops, I'd wager. How would you use those things, LT?"

Laybourne frowned.

"You'd drop as many of them as you could on your unsuspecting target and let them run free, killing and eating everything they came across before you moved in, wouldn't you?" Leon chuckled. "It'd be an easy means of cleaning out a planet's population before your own troops ever touched the ground."

Laybourne wanted to punch Leon and smash in the alien's too-perfect teeth but he managed to keep his anger under control. It wasn't Leon's fault that his mind was fast as his body. If anything, Laybourne supposed he should be on his knees thanking God that Leon was on his side.

"Could be he's right," Robinson added. "I say we head for the *Cerebus* too. If Leon *is* right, there ain't no indigenous population worth speaking of for us to make contact with at this point anyway and the colonel's plan is seriously FUBARed, LT."

Weighing the options of continuing on towards the city or heading back, Laybourne finally had to admit that retreat might just be the thing that was called for in their current situation. The *Cerebus* offered not only a secure location to regroup and fully reassess their mission but also a means to escape this forsaken world too if it came to that.

"Okay," Laybourne conceded. "We'll make for the *Cerebus.* You've convinced me. Let me make it clear though that this isn't a democracy. I'm in command here until either one of those monsters tears me apart, got it?"

"Yes, sir!" Leon, Hardtower, and T'chal said in chorus.

Sergeant Robinson merely nodded. "Of course, the question is how do we get back? If those things can take out a squad of mechs, we're sure not gonna be much of a challenge for them."

"Oh ye of little faith," Leon quipped. "Are we not the Hell's Banshees?"

Private Hardtower of all people spoke up next. The private's voice almost squeaked as he said, "Maybe the squad of mechs drew the bulk of those things out there away. I mean, it sure had to take a lot of them to stop the Blackwings, right?"

Leon shook his head. "I wouldn't count on that first part. Like I said, if the Kep'at are using things are planet clearers, there's really no telling how many of those monsters we're dealing with. Could be millions of the things."

"Millions?" Hardtower croaked.

"Regardless, we're all ignoring the question of why they haven't come after us in here," Laybourne reminded the others. "Is there something special about this house?"

"Could be those things are just holding us here until their bosses show up, LT," Leon said.

"That would make sense," Robinson hurriedly agreed. "It's what I would have those things do if I were using them like the Kep'at seem to be."

"That will make our getting away from this place much harder," T'chal grumbled, joining the conversation in his own simple way.

"We still have to do it though, LT." Robinson took a step closer to him as Laybourne continued to stare out the bedroom window. "You know we do. If we stay here, we're dead."

Laybourne nodded. "Get everyone ready. We'll head out at dawn."

"Wait up a second!" Robinson said. "Why are we hoofing it? I assume you have a good reason for not just calling in a dropship."

"Yeah, I do. The *Cerebus* doesn't have any. All the colonel gave us were some attack birds. Even with our reduced numbers, they couldn't carry us all even if both of them came. Not to mention, we're trying to keep a low profile," Laybourne explained.

"I'd wager the detonation of that mech's power core was a pretty loud sign that we're here," Robinson countered.

"If the Kep'at are here already and paying attention, maybe, but even if they did pick it up, they may not know who and what they're up against yet. Putting those birds in the air will tip them off it's the Banshees on their doorstep for sure. We can't risk. And before any of you ask, we can't risk the tanks that are supposed to be gearing up either. Sergeant, contact the ship and have them stand down."

"Sir?" Robinson asked.

"You heard me, Sergeant. If those things can take out a squad of mechs, there is no reason to suspect that they might not be able to handle the tanks as well. We can't afford to risk them to save our butts. We're going to need them if and when the Kep'at show themselves."

"Understood, sir," Robinson said and walked away to carry out his orders, already in the process of opening a channel, via the link in his combat helmet, to the *Cerebus.*

****

Laybourne and the other survivors of his platoon settled in for the night. It was going to be a long one. Every so often, if he looked closely, Laybourne could see the dirt moving and shifting outside the house through the bedroom window as the monsters moved about beneath it. They were certainly still out there and waiting. Waiting for what, he didn't really know.

Leon was asleep next to the bedroom's door, his rifle clutched in his hands and lying across his chest for quick use if need be. T'chal had sacked out across the room, Leon and his massive body were propped up against the wall. Laybourne had sent Sergeant Robinson and Hardtower to check on the other Banshees in the bedroom across the hall and get them up to speed on the plan come morning.

Laybourne knew he should try to get some rest too but couldn't. All these men and women with him were his responsibility and it weighed on him heavily. He shrugged his backpack from his shoulders, setting it on the floor, to dig through it. He found a stim and depressed it against the side of his neck. It gave a hiss as it injected its contents into his bloodstream. Laybourne wasn't a fan of stims. They could make a person sloppy if they weren't used correctly and he couldn't afford that now. He couldn't afford to pass out from exhaustion in the middle of a crisis either though. Shooting himself up was the lesser of two evils as he saw things.

A fresh wave of energy washed over him as the stim did its work. His heart pumped harder inside his chest and his mind grew sharper. He knew the feeling wouldn't last long so he wanted to make the best use of it he could. Stepping over Leon, he quietly left the bedroom and headed downstairs.

The living room was even darker than the bedrooms upstairs. Its windows didn't allow in as much ambient starlight as the ones upstairs did. He paused at the bottom of the stairs allowing a moment for his eyes to adjust.

Preston saw him and came rushing over. The man was a wreck. He was on edge and looked as if every nerve in his body was frayed. Laybourne wondered if Preston had popped some stims of his own but then realized that it was most likely Barta's condition that affected the man so heavily.

"Those things are still out there, sir," Preston informed him. "We've been able to hear them moving about quite a bit. None of them have risked trying to get into the house through the doors or windows yet though. I think they know what will happen to them if they do."

"Calm down, trooper." Laybourne reached out, resting a hand on Preston's shoulder. "I've got a plan and we're getting out of here when the sun comes up."

That seemed to relieve Preston some but his edge quickly returned as Laybourne's words fully struck him. "What about Barta, sir? Johnny says we can't move her."

Laybourne raised a hand, silencing Preston as he turned to look at Barta and Johnny. Barta was exactly where she had been the last time he saw her, lying in a puddle of her own sweat and blood on the living room's couch. Johnny sat in the floor next to the couch, keeping a close eye on her and her condition. He was running a handheld version of a med-scanner over her as Laybourne moved to approach him.

"Well?" Laybourne asked, standing over the medic.

"You can rest easy, sir, in regards to what those things out there might be carrying, a scratch or bite from them can be deadly yes but not as fast as it's happening to her." Johnny nodded at Barta. "She's pregnant, sir. Didn't report it either. Heck, she might not even have known it's in such early stages."

Laybourne's eyes bugged. "Seriously?"

"Yes, sir," Johnny assured him. "If I hadn't been running such deep scans looking for little presents left by the tentacles that tore her up so bad, I might have missed it too. Her condition is interacting with the bacteria on those things' tentacles and speeding up the decay in living tissue they appear to cause."

"I would think something like being pregnant would be an easy thing to spot son," Laybourne challenged the young medic.

"Normally so, sir, you're right, but this child's father wasn't human." Johnny shifted where he sat, clearly uncomfortable delivering the information that he was.

Laybourne shot a glance at Preston. The man was turning red at this news but so far appeared to be keeping whatever rage he must be feeling in check.

"The baby appears to have more biological characteristics of its father than it does its human mother. Its bio-energy acts as sort of a cloak if you will," Johnny explained. "That's why her condition was so hard to detect."

Laybourne swallowed hard. He knew of only race that had characteristics like that and that meant this child's real daddy was asleep in the upstairs bedroom above them. "Damn," he muttered under his breath. This was the last thing he needed right now.

He glanced over at Preston again and saw that the private had put two and two together himself as well. Preston was shaking where he stood but held his ground like the professional soldier he was instead of charging up the stairs.

Laybourne quickly shifted the subject, though he knew nothing he said or did was going to take Preston's mind off the fact that he wasn't the baby's father. "So you're saying the rest of us are safe from this type of infection then?"

"Yes and no," Johnny told him. "A wound from one of those things will kill you if untreated but nowhere near as fast as this. I would suggest not letting them get in hand-to-hand combat range."

Stifling a laugh, Laybourne rubbed at his cheeks with the fingers of his right hand. "Right. I'll keep that in mind."

Laybourne knelt down next to Johnny and whispered carefully, "Is there anything you can do for her and the baby?"

Johnny shook his head sadly. "They were dead the moment she was infected, sir. It's just a matter of time now."

"Does Preston know that?" Laybourne kept his voice as low as possible.

Johnny shrugged. "I think he does but he isn't ready to admit it or maybe isn't capable of coping with it yet."

"We're moving out when the sun comes up," Laybourne told Johnny, his voice gruff and hard.

Johnny nodded his understanding as Laybourne got to his feet.

Laybourne figured there was not going to be an easy means of dealing with Preston short of letting the man have a go at Leon and Leon spilling his guts all over the house's floor.

"Sir!" Preston started in the second Laybourne was on his feet. "I'm not leaving Barta behind, sir."

Barta moaned at that exact that moment. It was moan of such great pain that even Laybourne flinched at the sound of it. Preston appeared on the edge of tears, though his stance was a strong and proud one.

"We don't have any choice, soldier," Laybourne pitied the man but there was nothing he could for him. "You know she's dead already and we can't put everyone else at risk by trying to carry her with us."

"You're just saying that because that freak upstairs is your friend. I should have known you'd be trying to clean up his messes for him."

"Watch it, Private!" Laybourne roared. "There's no room for personal feelings in our line of work. I'm doing my bloody job and that's all."

"We're not leaving her here to die with those things. You know what they'll do to her when we're gone!" Preston raged.

And Laybourne did know. He, too, had seen the monsters eating the fallen members of his platoon.

"Johnny, can you make her death an easy one?"

Both Preston and Johnny stared at him in shock at the question. Finally, Johnny nodded. "Of course, LT."

"She'll go out as peacefully as she can, Preston. Johnny will see to that after you had some time with her. And we'll burn the house behind us as we leave. That's all I can offer you in terms of comfort, soldier, though I am sorry for your loss."

Tears were pouring over Preston's cheeks as he answered through gritted teeth, "Thank you, sir, but don't think this makes me and that alien freak upstairs even because it doesn't."

"I'll pretend I didn't hear that for your sake, Private," Laybourne said. "I understand what you must be feeling right now. We've all lost people. Again, it's part of the job. Going after Leon though is a really bad idea. Your chances would be better with those monsters out there and you know it."

Preston kept silent as Laybourne gave Johnny a nod of thanks and then headed back up the stairs the house's second floor.

****

The Ventari VII night broke as the sun rose over the distant hills. Laybourne and the rest of the surviving members of his platoon gathered in the house's living room. Johnny had dealt with Barta two hours earlier. He and Preston had moved her body into the house's kitchen and covered it on the floor there. Laybourne saw that doing so had taken a great toll on Preston. The soldier sat on the blood-stained couch, staring out the front window. Not even Leon's presence had roused the man from the funk of his loss. Laybourne couldn't even begin to imagine what it felt like to find out you were going to be a dad, find out the child wasn't yours, and then lose both it and your lover all in the same night. If he could have, he would have suspended Preston from his duties but as things stood, Preston, like the rest of them, had no choice but press on if he wanted to stay alive. Laybourne wasn't really sure that Preston did, but he wasn't going to abandon the man if there was any other choice.

As to Leon, if Barta's death bothered him at all, the alien didn't show it. Laybourne wondered that if Leon knew if Barta had been carrying his child when she died would have changed things. It wasn't his place to get involved though. Johnny appeared smart enough to keep his mouth shut too. Things that happened between Banshees behind closed doors stayed there unless it directly affected the mission ahead of them. And this matter didn't unless Preston was a fool. No one in their right mind, except maybe Colonel Hell, would pick a fight with Leon. Some of the Banshees back when Laybourne was just a corporal had come to call Leon "Death Walker" and with good reason.

Laybourne appraised his men. All of them were tired and on edge from the unexpected attack by the things outside the day before. The long night of being trapped in this house and losing Barta hadn't helped things either. He wondered again if he should relent and call in the tanks aboard the *Cerebus* for support but he knew he couldn't risk losing them too. If his platoon didn't make it back, Captain Pulliman would assume command and make whatever calls needed to be made to carry out the company's mission as best he could. If they lost the tanks though, and the Kep'at showed up in force, they were all royally and truly screwed. The odds of a single company making a real stand against the size of the Kep'at force that Laybourne feared was inbound for the planet, or maybe already here, were bleak even with the tanks. The sheer firepower of the three tanks though would allow them to hold out a lot longer, maybe even long enough for the colonel to arrive and kick some Kep'at tail.

Sensing his men were growing impatient, Laybourne snapped into action. "Leon, you have point. Everybody else, fall in. We're moving out. Double time!"

The noises of the creatures outside moving through the ground had slacked off and Laybourne hoped that meant some of the things had wandered away during the night.

Leon led with Hardtower and Sergeant Robinson following on his heels. Everyone else spread out in a long line behind them. In less than half a minute of leaving the house, the creatures showed themselves. One of the monsters leaped upwards from the dirt at Leon. Leon swiped his rifle around in front of him, smashing its butt into the side of the monster's head. The monster sprawled sideways out of Leon's path as the lithe alien kept moving. Robinson fired two rounds from his rifle into the downed monster's chest as he passed it to make sure the thing wouldn't be getting back up.

More of the monsters made their play as the Banshees ran on towards the trees. One sprang up directly in the path of the Banshee named Stephenson. Stephenson crashed into the monster unable to bring up his weapon or even stop himself before the impact. The Banshee and the monster toppled onto the ground with Stephenson on top. Stephenson's rifle was useless, wedged between their two bodies. The Banshee went for his sidearm but never got to use it. By the time the weapon had cleared the holster on his hip, the monster's whipping tentacles had arced around behind him to plunge into and through his back. That was the last Laybourne saw of the Banshee, though he heard the gargling noise that passed for the man's final scream behind him as he ran.

Another Banshee went down as a tentacle shot out of the dirt and wrapped itself around the woman's right ankle. She hit the dirt hard, shattering her nose from the impact, as the rest of the creature's body followed that first tentacle to the surface. As it rose up from the ground, the woman was ready. She had twisted her body around to angle the barrel of her rifle at the emerging monster. Her finger held back her weapon's trigger sending a stream of automatic rounds into the thing's upper body. The monster jerked about as the bullets ripped through it then flopped over to move no more, its yellow blood staining the grass and dirt beneath it.

For a moment, Laybourne allowed himself to hope that woman was going to make it. That hope died as two tentacles exploded out of the dirt, one on each side of where she sat, and wrapped around her. They yanked her to lay flat against the ground as she struggled to break free of them. A third tentacle came bursting upwards through the center of her body in a spray of red blood that shot into the air and then splattered down over her twitching form like rain.

Laybourne turned his eyes away and moved to follow the others of his platoon into the trees. As he reached the trees, Leon was there waiting on him. The alien had stopped and turned to open fire into the ranks of monsters that were all above ground now and chasing the Banshees on foot.

Leon's carefully aimed fire dropped the two closest of the monsters who were snapping at the slowest of the Banshees' heels.

Leon's first burst split the skull of the first monster like an axe blade. His second sent the other monster reeling as Leon's bullets gouged a gaping hole in its chest, severing several of the thing's tentacles from its body in the process.

It took Laybourne a moment to realize the last Banshee still running for the trees was T'chal. He cursed himself for not remembering just how slow the powerhouse of man moved. Not that T'chal was a man. He was an alien like Leon, the only other one in the platoon Laybourne had led into this mess.

Laybourne could see that T'chal wasn't going to make it in time. He motioned for the other Banshees to keep moving as fast as they could. Leon ignored him and held his ground, continuing to pour fire into the monsters closing on T'chal. Laybourne couldn't blame him. Both of them had known T'chal a long time. The big alien was likely the closest thing Leon had to a real friend.

"You go!" Laybourne shouted at Leon. "I'll cover him!"

Leon shook his head, casting aside his empty rifle to draw matching pistols from the holsters on his boots. The alien spun the weapons on his fingers as he brought them to bear on the monsters that had overtaken T'chal.

T'chal was putting up one heck of a fight of his own. The big alien impaled one of the monsters with the barrel of his rifle, shoving it through the thing like a spear. One monster jumped at T'chal from his right side and went down from a series of well-placed, cracking shots from Leon's pistols. Another jumped at T'chal from his left. The big alien caught it, midflight, his thick fingers sinking into its body from the sheer strength his hands met it with. T'chal lifted the alien over his, tearing it apart along its middle with a massive heave. The monster's entrails and yellow blood splattered down over him before he tossed the two pieces of the monster in different directions.

Laybourne dropped still another monster coming at T'chal, emptying half his rifle's mag into the thing in a single, long burst of fire. The monster was flung off its feet by the barrage and went flying several feet backwards.

There were just too many of the monsters though. Even with Leon and himself laying down heavy fire on them to keep them from getting at T'chal, they managed to swarm the big alien. T'chal disappeared under a wave of purple bodies and writhing tentacles.

"No!" Laybourne heard Leon screaming. He saw Leon holster his pistols to draw his knives and knew he had to stop him. Laybourne came bounding up to Leon's side and threw himself into Leon's path, body-checking him with his rifle.

"He's dead, Leon!" Laybourne yelled. "We have to leave him!"

Leon's snarl was feral and utterly inhuman as he met Laybourne's eyes. Laybourne felt a chill shoot through him. It was as if he was staring directly into the eyes of death itself. Leon relented though. He shoved Laybourne away and turned to run towards the trees without looking back.

****

Captain Pulliman sat in his command chair on the bridge of the *Cerebus*. He was aware of First Lieutenant Laybourne's plight, keenly aware, but even so, it was the least of his worries at the moment. In the last few minutes, his sensor tech had picked up numerous FTL jumps into the Ventari system. There were now over a dozen Kep'at vessels approaching Ventari VII and the jumps hadn't stopped either. Worse, several power sources, clearly of Kep'at technology, had come alive on the planet's surface. The Kep'at were here. The bastards had been waiting on them when they arrived.

Ventari VII wasn't a trap the Kep'at had intentionally set for the Banshees as far as Captain Pulliman could tell. It was working out to be a deadly one anyway though. The *Cerebus* was mostly powered down and under cloak so unless the Kep'at already on the planet had seen her land, she should be safe, but she certainly couldn't make a run for it if that changed. Trying to punch through the Kep'at forces that would be in orbit and stationed in system by the time Laybourne and his men returned, if they returned, would be impossible. Pulliman heavily considered pulling out and leaving Laybourne behind. Doing so would be a justifiable call on his part. He couldn't bring himself to give that order though. Even if the *Cerebus* dropped her cloak and made for orbit this instant, there was no guarantee that she could outrun the Kep'at ships already in system and she certainly couldn't outfight them. The *Cerebus* was a tough ship, but at fifteen-to-one odds and four of those fifteen being full-size Kep'at battleships. . .

There was also the matter of Laybourne himself to consider. The first lieutenant was in Colonel Hell's favor. If Pulliman returned without Laybourne, it might cost him his command. The colonel was infamous for fits of fury that had ended the careers of countless Banshees who had made the wrong call. Leaving Laybourne behind wouldn't necessarily be the wrong call to make given the circumstances but could he risk Colonel Hell viewing it that way? No, all he could do was wait for Laybourne to make it back to the ship and perhaps the two of them together might come up with a plan to get the Hell off the planet before things got any worse.

Pulliman put his tactical officer onto coming up with some strategies on how the *Cerebus* might get through the Kep'at blockade once it was fully in place. He didn't dare risk firing off a messenger drone to the colonel aboard the *Hellhound*. The risk of being detected if he did so was too great. The *Hellhound* was in route to Ventari VII via Void Drive rather than an FTL jump, but Pulliman didn't really think the great ship was in any real danger by the Kep'at forces present. Colonel Hell didn't get where he was by being stupid. The *Hellhound*'s long-range sensors would detect the Kep'at and give the ship and her crew plenty of warning about what was waiting on them here. Besides, the colonel had planned on fighting his way into the system to extract the *Cerebus*. The colonel had foreseen the Kep'at being in the process of trying to take Ventari VII when the *Hellhound* arrived.

"Are you well, sir?" Pulliman's first officer, Lifeson, asked.

Pulliman jumped in his seat. He quickly settled himself and looked over at Lifeson who stood between where he sat and the ship's helm. "I'm fine."

"Our situation has become unexpectedly dire," Lifeson commented without emotion.

Pulliman sighed. Leave it to an android to state the obvious and Lifeson was one. He had been Pulliman's first officer since he took command of the *Cerebus*. The two of them had worked together a long time, but Lifeson's appearance still got to Pulliman sometimes. Lifeson was utterly human in every sense of the word in terms of his appearance except for the fact that his skin was a deep, bluish-green hue. Lifeson's voice and mannerisms, though, were anything but human. His voice sounded just as machine as Peart was on the inside. Lifeson was a great asset to the ship, no one could argue that, but Pulliman sometimes wished he had a human first officer.

"Yes, it has," Pulliman agreed. "Does that wired brain of yours have any suggestions?"

"Not at this time," Lifeson replied. "I believe that the course of action you have chosen in opting to wait for First Lieutenant Laybourne's return instead of attempting flight is the best one available at this time."

Pulliman grunted. "Glad you approve."

Lifeson nodded. "There has been no communication with Laybourne and the remnants of his platoon since they began their journey back to the *Cerebus*. That said, Laybourne is a competent officer and there is no need for any great concern yet, given that we are under orders to maintain comm silence if possible."

"You believe Laybourne will make it back then?" Pulliman asked.

"That remains to be seen. We have no real data on the obstacles he is facing beyond his reports of the planet being occupied by subterranean, carnivorous aliens who apparently present in great numbers."

Pulliman leaned forward in his command chair. "Do you believe these creatures are a threat to us here aboard the *Cerebus?*"

"Not at this time, Captain," Lifeson answered. "It is highly unlikely that such beings could do any measurable damage to a ship like this one. I have, however, taken precautions as per protocol. We can't raise our shields, as you are fully aware, nor can we rely on the ship's auto-defense system. Doing either would surely alert the Kep'at to our presence. I have, however, ordered all the airlocks sealed and posted guards at them."

Pulliman wasn't ready to attempt that the creatures Laybourne had reported could be a threat to his ship either. Still, it worried him that the things had taken out a squad of mechs. He made a mental note not to underestimate the creatures just because they seemed primitive and unarmed by modern standards then turned his attention once again to the FTL jump data his sensor tech was directing to his personal screen on the arm of his chair. Two more Kep'at warships had just jumped in system. He could only wonder how many more were coming.

****

Laybourne slumped against the alien tree. The tree was a twisted and peculiar-shaped thing that resembled a three-pronged pitchfork reaching for the sky of Ventari VII. His whole body ached and his muscles were pushed to their limits. He couldn't even guess at how long he and his platoon had been running through the woods, but it felt like hours. It took effort to catch his breath and wipe the sweat from where his hairline met the bottom of the combat helmet he wore.

Of all the Banshees who had set out from the house when the sun rose only Leon, Hardtower, Johnny, Preston, and himself were left. The others had died horrible deaths being ripped apart by the monsters that were very much likely still after them. The platoon's survivors hadn't been attacked in sometime, but that didn't mean they had lost the creatures or that they had given up. Another attack could come at any second and they all knew it. There was no way to predict when or where the monsters would hit them since the things traveled underground.

As Laybourne leaned on the tree, Hardtower, Preston, and Johnny lay sprawled out in the grass. Each of them looked to be in just as rough of shape as he was himself. Only Leon stayed on his feet unaided. The lithe alien's eyes scanned the area around them as he sniffed at the air. Even Leon's heightened senses were next to useless against the foe they faced.

Leon's race didn't sweat like humans but instead emitted an odor that reminded Laybourne of Earth honey when they pushed themselves. The air around Leon smelt sickly sweet as he walked towards where Laybourne was.

"We can't stop here, sir," Leon told him.

"The rest of us need a minute, Leon. It's that or stop altogether," Laybourne managed to rasp.

"I understand that sir but. . ."

Laybourne hauled himself up, standing on his own again. "Give me your medkit," he ordered.

With a look of confusion, Leon shrugged his backpack from his shoulders and dug out his kit. He tossed it over.

Laybourne took out the standard-issue stim injector inside it and depressed it to the side of his neck. He felt fire flowing through his veins as the stimulants swan into his system.

Leon's expression was one of concern as Laybourne handed him his kit back.

"Those are dangerous, sir," Leon said, trying to hide the pity that still managed to creep into his voice and failing.

"He's right, sir," Johnny chimed in.

"Leave it be," Laybourne ordered the two of them. "Everyone else, shoot up too. We're all going to need the energy. We've got a good distance left to cover."

Hardtower and Preston shot up as quickly as they could dig out their own stim injectors. Johnny didn't.

"I really don't think this is a good idea, sir," Johnny said.

"I didn't ask you, Johnny. Keep your medical opinions to yourself until I do, understood?"

"Yes, sir," Johnny said, shooting up as well.

Everyone was on their feet again and getting ready to move out when the next attack came.

The ground in front of Laybourne bulged then came flying at his face as one of the creatures exploded from it. Laybourne screamed, whipping his rifle around at the creature like a club. Its butt caught the monster along the side of its head and sent it careening sideways.

Hardtower wasn't so lucky. Three of the monsters stuck at him at once. Hardtower managed to pump one of them full of lead, splattering the thing's yellow blood over himself in the process, before the other two sunk the tips of their primary tentacles into him. Hardtower howled as the monsters jerked him from his feet and fell onto him. The tiny mouths running the lengths of the underside of their tentacles gnawed on the armor of his combat gear and removed chunks of his exposed flesh. Hardtower struggled against them, his rifle lost as he hit the ground. His right hand fought to reach the pistol holstered on his hip. He never got the chance to grab it. One of the creature's main mouth on what passed for its face intercepted his hand, biting it off at the wrist.

Red blood sprayed from the stump that was now the end of Hardtower's arm.

Preston let loose the rage pent up within him on the two monsters that came for him. He bashed in the head of the first with three quick blows from the butt of his rifle and then spun it around in his hands to fire point blank into the second. Its back disappeared in a blast of exit wounds before its lifeless body flopped down into the hole it had emerged from.

Leon was on his game as usual, tossing his rifle aside and drawing one of his pistols. He shoved its barrel into the open maw of the closest monster coming from him and squeezed the trigger. The thing's head exploded in a shower of yellow pulp. His left foot lashed out, catching a second monster just beneath its chin, snapping its head at an unnatural angle with the sound of shattering bone. A third monster was stupid enough to close with him. Leon smacked it across its face with his pistol, dislocating its jaw. Before the monster could recover, he placed his pistol against the thing's forehead and calmly sent it to Hell.

Laybourne heard Johnny's cries for help as he finished the monster he was fighting by emptying half of his rifle's magazine into its stomach. He left it, oozing entrails and twitching where it lay, to run towards the medic.

Johnny was only up against one of the monsters or Laybourne could see the medic would have been dead already. Johnny wrestled with one of the creatures. They both had a firm hold on Johnny's rifle and fought over it between them as tentacles whipped at Johnny's head. Johnny jerked his head about, dodging them as Laybourne came up behind the creature and put a three-round burst into its spine. The monster shrieked, releasing its hold on Johnny's weapon. Johnny tumbled, losing his footing. He landed hard on his butt as Laybourne almost instantly yanked him to his feet again.

And then as quickly as it started, the battle was over. The bodies of eight of the monsters lay sprawled about the small clearing, Hardtower's mangled form resting with them. Leon had dealt with the two that had been making a quick meal of Hardtower's corpse.

Laybourne staggered, not sure if it was the stims or exhaustion that was catching up to him. Preston stepped to his side to help support him until he recovered.

"This changes nothing," Leon said. "We have to keep moving. If we stay here, we are as dead as Hardtower."

Laybourne nodded, shoving Preston away from him. "You heard the man, boys. Move!"

Leon led the others as they continued towards where the *Cerebus* waited on them.

****

The path Leon led them angled strangely through the woods. The sun had reached its peak in the sky of Ventari VII. Laybourne's nerves racked his brain with agony as he continued to push himself on. His heart was thundering in his chest as if it were going to burst. With the double dose of stims he had shot himself up within the last twenty four hours, he worried that it just might too.

They were getting close to where the *Cerebus* sat cloaked and the monsters' attacks were becoming more frequent and more desperate. The creatures clearly wanted to stop them before they made it to the ship. It was as if the things sensed that once they made it there, they would be beyond their reach. Laybourne hadn't figured out if the creatures themselves were intelligent yet or not. Sometimes they acted that way and others like nothing more than simple animals after food. His best guess was that the Kep'at were controlling them somehow and that control was either very limited or tended to cut in and out. He supposed it didn't matter. The monsters were lethal enough and then some regardless.

"Grenade!" Leon shouted as he flung one up ahead along the path that he was leading them on. The alien never slowed. He charged right on towards the blast of the grenade as it detonated. Laybourne and the others hit the dirt and then were on their feet again and running in as quickly as they could.

The blast turned a trio of monsters, above ground and waiting on them, into charred and tattered pieces of meat. Laybourne gave an unprofessional shout of victory that was cut short as a monster came charging at him from the trees to his left. He spun to meet it, leveling his rifle at its chest. His rifle clicked empty as he squeezed its trigger. Laybourne cursed as his eyes went wide and the monster plowed into him. The impact knocked him over as the monster grabbed a hold of him with several of its whipping tentacles and followed him to the ground. One tentacle slashed a deep grove of torn flesh along his forehead. The world spun around Laybourne as he tried not to blackout and another tentacle flung his rifle from his hands to go flying into the trees. A jarring jolt of pain as another tentacle stabbed into and through his left shoulder snapped him into action. Like a gunfighter from the Earth's past, he freed his pistol from the holster on his hip and smashed its butt upwards. He knocked the monster's head back and away from him as it tried to sink the rows of razor-like teeth inside its primary mouth into the side of his neck. Stunned, the creature hesitated just long enough for him get the barrel of his pistol up against the side of its body as the two of them wrestled. He fired into its body again and again. His pistol cracked four times before the monster's limp form slid off of him. Then Leon was there, standing over him. Leon extended a hand and he took it as the alien pulled him up.

"Johnny's gone," Leon told him then shoved him on along through the trees. "Now move!"

Laybourne stumbled onward, clutching at his shoulder. It leaked blood that soaked into the cloth of his shirt and ran in bright red rivers down his right arm and chest. He could see Preston had made it through the attack too. The man had taken point and was running like a bat out of hell, dodging low-lying tree limbs and jumping over bugles in the dirt that may or may not be more creatures rising to meet him. Laybourne knew Leon was behind him somewhere, making sure that he kept moving and stayed on his feet. He was glad the alien was there because he honestly didn't know how much more he had left in him.

****

His vision was blurry as Laybourne opened his eyes. He sat bolt upright in the bed he laid in, screaming. It was only after he felt Captain Pulliman's hands forcing him to lie back down that he realized he wasn't in the woods anymore. Somehow, he was aboard the *Cerebus.*

"What happened?" he croaked.

"According to Leon, you got knocked unconscious by one of those things out there. Apparently, you had killed it, but it was still moving just enough to get in a good blow to your skull.

Considering you already must have had a concussion at that time, it's a miracle you're not injured worse than you are," Captain Pulliman explained.

Laybourne noticed that Pulliman's first officer, the android Lifeson, was in the med-bay with them. There was no sign of Leon or Preston.

"The others?"

"Preston is dead. Not from those things out there though as I understand it. He attacked your man Leon shortly after they came aboard."

Laybourne found he couldn't help but laugh. Somewhere deep inside he had known it was just a matter of time until that would happen.

Lifeson cocked his head at the sound of his laughter. The android peered at him with sharp, radiant blue eyes. "Perhaps he is not yet ready for the discussion you wish to have with him, Captain."

"I'm fine, thank you," Laybourne growled, "aside from hurting like hell. Now tell me what's going on?"

Laybourne knew that for Captain Pulliman to be here at his bedside, something bad had to have happened.

"The Kep'at are here," Pulliman informed him.

"So?" Laybourne frowned. "We suspected that, didn't we?"

"You misunderstand," Lifeson quipped.

"They're here in force and out in the open now," Pulliman told him. "While you were fighting to stay alive, over two dozen Kep'at warships made FTL jumps in system. They've taken up defensive positions around Ventari VII."

Laybourne whistled. "We are truly screwed, aren't we?"

"Oh, it gets worse," Pulliman shook his head. "They're on the planet too just like we thought as well. Not long after the first ships jumped in, we detected quite a few power sources turning on around this continent. I don't believe they were waiting on us but none the less, they were apparently already here when we arrived."

Laybourne pushed himself up onto his elbows. His strength and sense of orientation was returning quickly. "Have they detected the *Cerebus*?"

Captain Pulliman shook his head though he looked worried. "Not yet as far as we can tell but it's only a matter of time. I've got our power signature as low as I can make it and our cloak is still engaged but even so. . ."

"I take it the ships around the planet are too many to punch through."

"They'd tear us apart the second we entered space," Pulliman answered grimly. "The *Cerebus* isn't the *Hellhound*."

"That's the real reason you waited on me to make it back," Laybourne commented like the professional soldier he was without any bitterness.

"Maybe I was hoping you would have a better plan than us just waiting on Colonel Hell to show up with the *Hellhound*'s batteries blazing." Pulliman grinned.

"Sorry to disappoint you, Captain," Laybourne chuckled. "But you're out of luck on that one. I got nothing."

****

Ensign Steph Anderson sat at the sensor station on the *Cerebus*'s bridge, popping her knuckles. It was a nervous tick she fell into times of stress. The situation on Ventari VII certainly qualified as that. The ship was outgunned and essentially surrounded by enemy forces. She had been in battles before and survived them. Space battles were nothing like this though, and she hated being grounded with every fiber of her being. All readings indicated the cloak was working perfectly. She had transferred data on it to her screen and took a peek at it herself so she could be sure. Signing up with the Hell's Banshees had saved her from a terrible childhood on Centauri Alpha. Doing so had let her see the stars. More than that, the Banshees had given her life purpose and given her a home. Her aptitude with computers and test scores kept her being a ground pounder and that was something she was forever thankful for.

She hadn't slept much since the *Cerebus* had landed on Ventari VII. The news of the monsters that were out there, *in* the planet, kept her awake. Steph knew she was safe from them aboard the ship rationally but that fact didn't stop her nightmares from haunting her.

With a sigh, she pulled herself out of her thoughts and refocused herself on her work. Captain Pulliman had her running constant passive, low-power scans of the area around the ship. Running such weak scans wasn't quite as bad as being blind but it was close. Still, if the Kep'at were able to detect the ship and decided to act against it, her scans would be the only advance warning the entire company had.

She ran a cycle of scans and found nothing. No sign of the Kep'at or the monsters creeping up on them. There was nothing in the surrounding woods and the trees and the skies were clear of any threat. Still, she worried she was missing something.

On a whim, Steph reconfigured the ship's sensor array to run a quick scan of what lay beneath the surface of the ground outside.

As the data from it hit the screen in front of her, it was all she could do not to scream. With trembling hands, she ran the scan again. The data was the same.

"Sir!" Steph shouted at Lieutenant Waid. He was in command of the bridge since both Pulliman and Lifeson were elsewhere at the moment.

The lieutenant came swaggering over to her station. "What is it, ensign?"

The two of them had never gotten along. Waid was far too by the book by her standards. He didn't fit in well with the Banshees for the most part. Before signing up with them, Waid had been an officer in the Alliance fleet. The Banshees might be one of the best merc outfits in known space, but they didn't operate in the sort of hardnosed method that the Alliance did.

"I think you better take a look at this," Steph told him.

Waid leaned over her shoulder to give the screen of the sensor station a glance. That glance changed to an all-out stare as he muttered, "What in the devil is that?"

The image was one of a massive cluster of lifeforms that almost looked to be clustered together in one giant heap which was spread out around the *Cerebus*. It was impossible to count the number of lifeforms without the help of the sensor station's systems and even that was only an estimated count, a very frightening one.

"It's an image of the area around the ship, sir," Steph explained. "I'm reading thousands, maybe more, the system can't even get an accurate count, of the monsters that First Lieutenant Laybourne engaged. They're all around us, sir."

Waid ran his finger through his receding hair as he continued to stare at the data on the screen.

"We need to report this to the captain at once," Steph urged him.

****

After a prolonged argument with his doctor, Laybourne had convinced the woman that he was fit for duty. It was an argument he had come close to losing until he threatened to splatter her brains all over the med-bay if she didn't clear him. At that point, she had given in, if reluctantly. In truth, he wasn't hurt that badly. He'd had far worse over the years. The bruises and cuts covering his body didn't bother him at all. That type of low-level pain he could easily live with. The only thing that did bother him was the wound he had taken to his shoulder when one of those monsters had rammed the tip of one of its primary tentacles through it. That hurt like hell. His arm with the wound was sore and he had more trouble than he liked moving it, but he could still hold and use a weapon and that was enough.

The doctor had his gear delivered to him and he was in the process of suiting up when the ship's alarm klaxons began to blare. Pulliman and his first officer, Lifeson, had left the med-bay only minutes before his argument with the doc. He wished they were here now. The navy com-links they wore kept them patched into the *Cerebus*'s systems so they could've told him what was going on.

Laybourne hurriedly finished pulling up his pants and started donning his combat armor. When he was done, he raced out of the med-bay and nearly collided with Leon in the hallway beyond it.

"Sorry," Laybourne apologized as the alien righted himself from where Laybourne had shoved him into the wall of the corridor.

With a growl, Leon glared at him. "Just watch yourself next time."

"What's going on?" Laybourne demanded as Leon took off at a run and he followed after him.

"Those monsters are attacking the ship," Leon informed him. "We got warning that was a massive hive of them just outside it one second and the next, those things were tearing at the hull!"

Laybourne's mind reeled as Leon's words sunk in. "They can't penetrate the hull of a ship like the *Cerebus,*" he argued, "It's just not possible!"

"Tell them that," Leon spat. "Last word I got was that they'd already breached the hull in several spots on the lower decks."

"God in heaven help us," Laybourne stammered. "How many of them are there?"

The two of them reached a lift as its doors slid open to admit them.

Leon keyed in their destination as he answered. "No idea. Thousands? Tens of thousands? I suspect the things have been gathering around and beneath the ship since she landed."

The lift kicked into motion, heading downwards to the ship's lowest deck.

"Better be ready," Leon warned him as the alien checked his own rifle.

Laybourne did the same, checking his rifle's mag and making sure it was set to automatic fire.

"It's that bad?"

"From the screaming I am hearing in my earpiece, I'd say it's worse than whatever you're thinking," Leon replied.

"Great," Laybourne quipped, raising his rifle . . . and then the doors of the lift slid open, admitting the two of them into Hell.

****

The bridge around Captain Pulliman was in a frenzy. Officers were barking reports that continued to pour in from all over the ship. Pulliman still couldn't really believe it was really happening but the monsters had breached the *Cerebus's* hull at multiple points on her lowest deck.

He called up an image of the *things* that had used to do it with. The creatures resembled earthworms and their "heads" were more like giant scythes than the heads of anything that should be able to burrow through the ground. He wounded if the smaller, humanoid creatures actually dug the tunnels of the worm like things to travel through. That was the only thing that made sense. The worm like things used their blade-shaped heads to strike the hull of the ship to slash through her hull. Their heads were like razored, battering rams. There was no way the worms were a natural thing. They had to be bred for just this purpose—to act like tanks for the humanoid monsters.

There were four of the worms in all and that had taken a serve toll on the *Cerebus's* structural integrity in the last fifteen minutes. Their relentless attacks had created entry points for the humanoid ones to get inside her. The entire lower deck was all but lost. There were scattered areas where Banshees continued to hold out but it didn't look good.

Aside from the lower deck, the humanoid monsters were actually scaling the sides of the ship and trying to force a means of entrance through her sealed airlock. So far, only two of those had been breached and his men, along with Laybourne's ground pounders, were fighting them back at those points.

Pulliman's greatest concerns were that the ship's cloak had been comprised by the attack and the structural damage. The Kep'at could clearly see her now on any sensor sweeps they ran of the area. He knew they would be coming soon too unless they were counting on the monsters to deal with them. And that was a distinct possibility. The state of the lower deck worried him just as much. He could have it sealed off with structural shields when the ship lifted but there was no guarantee that they would hold under the pressures of leaving Ventari VII's atmosphere when the time came. He imagined that would be sooner rather than later too.

"Main power online," his voice boomed across the bridge. "I want our shields up and all activate defenses engaged!"

As the shields engaged, Pulliman snickered watching two of the worm things cut in half as a sphere of energy formed around the ship. The remaining two now hammered on the shield rather than the ship's hull but he knew for sure there wasn't any chance of the things cutting through it.

A second later, the *Cerebus*'s mounted, anti-personal hulls weapons came to life. The spat a literal wall of rounds at the rate of 10,000 a second, into the two worms and swarm of humanoids that had gathered around her, ripping them into bloody pulp that stained the grass and dirt of the clearing she sat in.

"That'll teach you mothers to frag with the Banshees," he said under his breath, allowing himself a grin.

With the bulk of the enemies exterior forces decimated, he returned his attention to the situation on the lower deck. His first officer, Lifeson, was down there somewhere. He'd sent the android to assist with holding the lower deck when the attack on the *Cerebus* had started. Pulliman regretted doing so. He could surely use Lifeson here now. The android was the best engineer he had, though that wasn't Lifeson's job. Lifeson's artificial brain was even more advanced than the *Cerebus's* main computer and could run probabilities and simulations at an uncanny rate. Lifeson was far more likely to be able to discern how to deal with the breaches on the lower decks than he was. That was simple fact. There was no room for ego when the lives of your entire crew were depending on you to make the best call.

****

The lift doors parted to relieve a warzone. The lowest deck of the ship was its main hanger bay. The wide open area was filled with tentacled monsters engaged with Banshees, both ship personnel and his own men, who fighting to stay alive. Leon sprang the lift, fire from his rifle, hosing three monsters that came bounding towards it. His stream of fire separated an arm from the shoulder of one of the creatures and killed the other two instantly, reducing their torsos to bleeding, ragged mess of blown apart meat. The arm bounced across the hangar bay floor leaving spots of yellow pus where it struck. The monster that had lost its arm snarled and pushed itself on faster towards Leon.

Laybourne lost sight of Leon as he found himself engaged with a group of monsters of his own. Two of the creatures were closing in on him as he sprinted away from the lift into the heart of the battle that was being waged in the hangar bay.

He swung his rifle around to fire at the two monsters as he ran. The motion caused fiery spikes of pain to shoot through his wounded shoulder but he still got the job done. His rifle spat death at the monsters. The closer of the two took a dozen rounds to its upper body and went sprawling backwards. The second shrieked as the fire from his rifle dug into its groin. Laybourne didn't how the creatures reproduced or if they even had reproductive organs drawn up inside that area of their bodies, but he winced all the same at the sight of where his bullets caught struck the creature. Yellow blood flowed in rivers down the lengths of its legs as it stopped in its tracks, lifting its head upwards towards the ceiling, and its shrieks turned to dying wails.

Laybourne spotted one of the *Cerebus*'s sensor techs named Carlson and wondered what in the heck the man was doing in the hangar bay. The tech cowered, half hidden, between the legs of a Blackwing Mech, clutching a standard issue Navy sidearm.

There were three more Blackwing suits in the hangar bay. Two were standing, powered down and unmanned, next to the one Carlson cowered below. The other had apparently been brought into action only to be destroyed by the monsters. Its shredded metal form rested in the center of a vast circle of dead monsters.

None of the three tanks in the hangar were active. They sat as if they were great metal gods watching the bloodshed around them with amusement. Powering up the tanks would be a mistake inside the hangar anyway, Laybourne reminded himself as he considered trying to do so to one of them. A single, panicked shot from its main gun would create a whole new set of problems to deal with assuming anyone inside the hangar survived to face it.

A Banshee screaming like an old Earth Viking warrior was lying down some heavy fire into the creatures with a handheld, heavy-weapon version of a Blackwing cannon. Its three barrels whirred as they spun and a continuous rain of spent shell casing clattered onto the deck floor from the weapon. The cannon cut down row after row of the monsters, but they were still managing to press on towards it and would soon overtake the Banshee from the looks of things.

Laybourne thought about adding his fire to the man's but decided against it. The sensor tech needed his help more and a single rifle wouldn't make that much difference anyway if a heavy weapon wasn't holding the monsters at bay.

"First Lieutenant Laybourne!" Carlson cried as he rushed to the sensor tech. "You have to get me out of here! I have a family back on Denab V!"

"Shut up!" Laybourne snapped at him as he slid between the Blackwing's legs to join Carlson there. "I couldn't even get myself out of here if I tried."

A glance over his shoulder at the lift door confirmed his words. The monsters had swarmed it and were now trying to pry the doors open so they could climb into the rest of the ship.

Laybourne dropped one of the monsters that noticed the two of them in their hiding spot and rushed at them with a very lucky, unaimed shot to the thing's skull. Its brains went splashing over the floor of the hangar deck.

Taking a better look around the hangar bay, Laybourne saw the gaping holes where its walls bent inward that the creatures had entered through. He had no idea how the monsters had managed to wreck things so badly down here and didn't want to find out. He looked at Carlson and accepted the fact that there was nothing he could really do to help the man except try to lead him out but with the number of monsters inside the hangar bay, there was little hope of that.

"Look!" Laybourne shouted over the gunfire and monstrous shrieks around them at Carlson. "We need to get out of here but I can't protect you. You're on your own as soon as we break cover."

"You can't just leave me!" Carlson pleaded.

Laybourne ignored the sensor tech. "On three. . .two. . .one. . .GO!"

Laybourne darted back out into the heat of the battle with Carlson doing his bloody all best to keep up with him. It proved useless. One of the monsters swept up Carlson from behind as he ran, lifting him from the hangar bay floor with several of its tentacles. Others of its tentacles plunged up and inside Carlson snaking paths through his entrails as the sensor tech screamed in agony.

Blocking out the sounds of Carlson's cries, Laybourne ran by where the Banshee with the Blackwing Cannon had fallen and was being devoured a pack of monsters that were swarming over him. Laybourne wasn't sure where exactly he was running to. It looked as if most of the Banshees in the bay were dead or dying. There was no easily defensible position that he could see that he could make it to in time.

One of the monsters lurched into his path too quick for him to dodge it. One of its tentacles slapped his face, its tiny mouths and spurs drawing blood as it dragged across his cheek. Moving fast, Laybourne batted the thing's tentacles away from him with his rifle and then brought it around to fire a point blank burst into the monster. Gaping holes blossomed on its back as his rounds ripped through its body. Its mouth still worked, opening and closing in fury, as it toppled to the floor.

Laybourne looked up from the sight of its flopping corpse and figured he was dead. Two of the monsters were basically on top of him and there was no hope of fighting them both off before their flailing tentacles ended him.

Seemingly out of nowhere, the android, Lifeson, appeared. Lifeson grabbed one the things by the back of its neck, snapping the bone there in the process. He flung the instantly dead monster away with superhuman speed as the other turned on him. He met it with a punch that crunched the bones of its skull, caving them inward.

"This way!" Lifeson shouted at him and darted towards the right side of the vast hangar bay.

Laybourne started to follow Lifeson but he spotted Leon. The alien Banshee was taking on an entire pack of the monsters alone. Leon's rifle was gone. Whether it had been taken from him or simply ran out of ammo and had been discarded, Laybourne didn't know. Leon fought with his twin knives, hacking and slashing at the tentacles that whipped out to stab at him or make a grab for his arms and legs. The monsters had Leon surrounded and their circle closed ever tighter around him. Leon's movements were growing slower but the exhausted alien was still doing his damnedest to hold the creatures back.

Leon looked on the verge of collapse. Gashes left from the monsters' tentacles covered his body and one of his eyes was swollen shut. A tentacle made a stab at his chest. Leon met it with the blade of the knife he clutched in his right hand. The blade severed a foot-long section of the tentacle from its tip. The severed piece fell to the hangar floor at Leon's feet where it continued to writhe and twitch. Leon's victory lasted less than a fraction of a second as another tentacle caught him on the side of his skull, striking the lithe alien hard enough to send him spinning. Leon somehow caught himself and regained his balance, throwing one of his knives into the face of the monster that had struck him. The blade of the knife sunk deep into the monster's throat. The monster died, gargling its own blood as it collapsed.

Laybourne knew he couldn't leave Leon to die. He would never be able to live with himself if he did. Laybourne considered Leon a close friend and the alien had saved his life countless times before. He doubted his efforts would make any difference given the number of aliens Leon faced, but he owed it to Leon to try.

Lifeson forgotten, Laybourne raised his rifle, bracing it against his shoulder, and took careful aim at the creatures around Leon. His finger was tightening on the trigger when suddenly Lifeson was by his side again. With speed even greater than Leon's, the android shoved the barrel of Laybourne's rifle towards the hangar bay floor.

"No!" the android told him. "Your friend is dead. There is nothing we can do for him!"

Laybourne started to protest but Lifeson lifted him from the hangar's floor, slinging Laybourne over his shoulder and sprinted away from the sight of Leon's desperate battle.

"Leon!" Laybourne yelled as he struggled vainly against the android's hold on him. If the alien Banshee heard his cry, he gave no sign of it. Leon was consumed like a blood-maddened warrior with the battle he fought.

****

Captain Pulliman's feeling of triumph at stopping more of the creatures from getting aboard his ship was torn from him as Ensign Steph Anderson at the sensor station yelled, "Sir, we've got incoming!"

Pulliman clinched one of his hands into a fist and smashed it down on the arm of his command chair. "Kep'at?"

"Yes, sir," Anderson replied. "Fighters. Several dozen of them, closing fast."

"Take them with guns," he snarled at his weapons officer. "Main batteries, fire at will."

Sections of the *Cerebus*'s forward, upper hull parted and six barreled railguns rose up from them. They pivoted on their turrets, moving to engage the inbound Kep'at fighter craft.

The Kep'at fighters broke formation, swerving in the air, attempting to dodge the streams of death the *Cerebus* spit at them. A few of the fighter pilots were either lucky or skilled enough to do so but the bulk of the Kep'at fighters were reduced to exploding fragments of metal that slashed through the night sky like shooting stars.

Those that survived returned fire. Ship-killer missiles streaked from their wings towards the Banshee ship. The *Cerebus* met them with a strong pulse of EMCs and sent the bulk of them veering away wildly.

Electronic countermeasures were not the *Cerebus*'s only defense, however. Her railguns engaged the missiles as well and reducing the number that struck her to a single missile. It came in hard and fast, impacting against her shields. The ship rocked from the blast.

"Shields are holding, sir!" Anderson reported.

"Minor impact damage reported in a few forward sections, sir!" Lieutenant Waid added. "Nothing major."

"The ten surviving fighters are coming around for another pass, sir!" Anderson yelled.

Gregory, the weapons officer, shouted, "Taking them with guns now, sir! They won't get another chance to hit us!"

The *Cerebus*'s railguns spun to meet the fighters on their second approach. The sky flashed her batteries opened up on them. Explosion after explosion lit the sky as one by one the Kep'at fighter craft became balls of fire that popped off like a series of fireworks. Only two of the fighters managed another strike at the *Cerebus* before they were destroyed and her EMCs easily dealt with the missiles they were able to launch.

"The sky is clear!" Gregory informed Pulliman. "All enemy targets destroyed."

Pulliman slumped deeper into his command chair in relief. The short, fierce battle had gone better than it had any right to have done and he was thankful for it. He knew though that the Kep'at weren't going just give up. A few dozen fighters meant nothing to them considering the sheer amount of forces they had stationed on and above Ventari VII.

Colonel Hell had assigned two Valkyrie fighters to Pulliman's command and he wanted nothing more than to launch them now. He couldn't though, because his hangar bay was full of tentacle-covered monsters. Hell, he didn't even know if the pilots for the two Valkyries were still alive. Odds were that they were among the personnel and soldiers who were in the hangar bay when it was breached. That meant they were likely dead just like everyone else who had been down there when the monsters came pouring in.

"The Kep'at are hailing us, sir," his comm officer, Loriel, told him.

"Put them through," Pulliman ordered. If the Kep'at wanted to talk, he figured if nothing else, it would buy them all time.

The bridge's main screen was filled with the image of a Kep'at officer. Pulliman cringed at the sight. The Kep'at's beady red eyes narrowed beneath the horns adorning his skull as they zoomed in on him. The Kep'at wore a mask of dried human flesh over its scaly, lizard like face. It was impossible to tell if the skin it wore had belonged to a man or woman it was stretched so tight and badly deteriorated.

"I am War leader Taur'et of the great house Min'ar. By now, you must have detected the fleet we have in this system. You are cut off and surrounded. If you wish to live, I demanded your unconditional surrender at once," Taur'et roared.

"Pleased to meet you too," Captain Pulliman laughed, hiding the fear he felt. "I'm Captain Kevin Pulliman of the Hell's Banshee ship, the *Cerebus.* I imagine you've heard of us, yes?"

The lips of the human skin Taur'et wore over his own stretched to the point of tearing as it was his turn to laugh. It was a sickening sound that chilled Pulliman to his very core.

Finally, Taur'et responded. "I have heard of the Hell's Banshees. You are not even real Alliance soldiers. You are scum. Fools who have no honor and sell your blades to whoever pays the highest."

"So you have heard of us." Pulliman feigned a smile.

"It does not matter if you are Alliance or not. You are human and therefore a threat to our interests here. Again, power down your ship's systems and prepare to be boarded or you will be destroyed," Taur'et growled.

"Wait!" Pulliman raised a hand towards the image of Taur'et on the view screen. "As you yourself admit, we are mercenaries. Perhaps, we can reach and an agreement that serves both our needs without further bloodshed."

"I have you surrounded and outgunned human. Even now, our *Feeders* are rampaging through your ship. What need have I of making any arrangement?"

"Your *Feeders*?" Pulliman asked.

Again, Taur'et laughed. "You have five standard minutes to power down your systems, little human, or you shall very much regret it."

With that, Taur'et terminated his message.

Lieutenant Waid, Ensign Anderson, and the other members of the bridge crew all stared at him as Pulliman shook his head. He hesitated a moment then barked, "Get this ship flight ready. I don't care what it takes. Just do it."

****

Laybourne and Lifeson fought their way across the hangar bay. The tentacle-covered monsters they were engaged with had finally forced open the doors of the lift leading out of the bay and were pouring up its shaft towards the higher decks of the *Cerebus*. That was really bad for the rest for the rest of the ship but great from them. The number of monsters in the bay had thinned greatly because of it. Still, getting through what was left in their path was far from an easy thing.

Lifeson carried no weapon, relying on his android strength and speed. Laybourne had discarded his rifle after running out of magazines for it. He'd used his only grenade as well, killing well over a half dozen of the tentacled creatures with it. He was down to his last two mags for his pistol now and could only pray they would be enough to see him though. The pistol lacked both the stopping power and level of penetration of his rifle. It took nearly an entire mag or an extremely well-aimed burst of shots to bring one of the monsters down with it. If it wasn't for Lifeson, he would have been swarmed and ripped apart by the creatures already.

The two of them reached the far side of the bay from where they had started and Laybourne saw why Lifeson had led them in this direction at once. There was a maintenance hatch on the wall. Laybourne felt his mouth drop open in awe as Lifeson took hold of the hatch's cover and yanked it open with his bare hands.

"Get in!" the android first officer ordered him.

Laybourne fired a final burst of fire at the monsters charging towards them and then dove through the open cover of the hatch. Lifeson followed him inside, slamming the hatch's cover back into place behind them.

"I'll hold them out," Lifeson told him. "I need you to go to that control panel over there and reroute the ship's power *through* the floor of the hangar. Do you understand?"

Lifeson said it all in his normal metallic tone without a hint of worry or panic that the things would get past him or that Laybourne might not know how to carry out the order he had been given.

"Yes, sir!" Laybourne flung the android a mock salute. "I fully support this plan!"

Laybourne's flippant humor was his means of coping with the utter terror he was feeling.

Lifeson gave what passed for a grunt as the monsters reached the hatch and began trying to push their way inside. "I cannot hold them long," Lifeson told him. "I suggest you hurry."

And Laybourne did. He didn't know a lot about ship systems but he would be damned if he wasn't about to learn them fast. Laybourne looked over the controls on the panel in front of him and did his best to reroute the power. He keyed what he hoped were the correct sequences into the panel and shouted, "Done!"

In the next instant, the entire hangar outside the hatch was filled with the echoing cries of the monsters as they were cooked alive by electrical currents that ran through the very floor they stood on. Lifeson jerked and shook where he held the hatch against them, as they died, the current running through his synthetic body as well. When the cries grew silent, Laybourne quickly switched the power back to flow along its normal routes. As he did, Lifeson toppled from his feet, crashing onto the floor.

Laybourne rushed to his side, kneeling next to him. Lifeson was gone though. Whatever passed for life inside his artificial body had left it. Smoke rose from his still-twitching form and Laybourne decided not to risk touching the android. He backed away from Lifeson and moved deeper into the maintenance shaft, searching for another way out of it. Spotting a ladder leading upwards, Laybourne sprang onto it, pistol in hand, and began to climb.

****

The dark red colors of Void Space swirled around the fast moving shape that was the *Hellhound* as she raced towards Ventari VII. She could have arrived in the Ventari systems instantly via FTL jump but Colonel Jerimiah didn't believe in taking unnecessary risks. Everything pointed towards the Kep'at having an active presence in the system and a FTL jump not only meant the *Hellhound* entering the system blind but also it would leave her crew and sensors disoriented for a brief moment. A moment like that could cost lives if the Kep'at were indeed already there. That was why he had elected to approach the system via the Void instead. Traveling as such was an old school method but it had its advantages in times like this.

Colonel Hell had relieved Captain Jordon and taken direct command of the *Hellhound* himself. Jordan was one of Hell's best captains but even so, Hell wanted to deal with this operation personally. There was too much at stake to risk anything else. He sat in the command car, watching the shifting hues of red ahead of the ship on the forward view-screen. Major Page stood to his right, hands clasped behind his back, waiting patiently, for their arrival in the Ventari system and whatever it might bring.

Hell rubbed at his chin with the fingers of his right hand, running multiple simulations of what may lie ahead through his mind. He was not an android or any other type of synthetic lifeform. His mind merely operated on that level, a gift from his DNA. Hell had never encountered another member of his race and knew as little about his own origins as his Banshees did. His whole life he had simply been able to function at a much higher cognitive level than anyone else he had ever met. It was more than just crunching numbers and running data through his head though. Hell had an almost supernatural edge over his enemies in any given battle because he could *feel* what they were feeling and knew what they were going to do next. It wasn't true precognition nor was it telepathy. It was just a part of who and what he was.

"Long-range sensor scan data coming in now, sir," Lieutenant Helena Vetal informed him from the bridge's sensor station.

"Feed it directly to my personal screen," he ordered her.

A display screen of pure energy flickered into existence before Hell's eyes. Upon on it formed the single star of the Ventari system and then the planets that orbited it. Hell gave the screen a mental command through the implant embedded in his temples and watched his view of the system shrink down to become a detailed look at the planet of Ventari VII. Around it were over two dozen Kep'at warships. He breathed a sigh of relief as he saw that none of them were super dreadnought class vessels. Most of them were destroyers acting as a screen for the four battleships present in the system. Amidst their numbers were also four heavy transports, larger than vessels of that class Hell had ever encountered before. The transports were of an odd shape and configuration as well. There was just enough Kep'at tech aboard the alien ships to make them register as Kep'at vessels but clearly they were alien ships. Originally, sub-light ones from the appearance of their hulls. The Kep'at must have upgraded them with their own drive technology.

Hell studied the hulls of the displayed unknown vessels carefully, his supernatural intuition kicking in. The race the ships belonged to was most likely a very primitive one . . . very animalistic in nature. The bulk of the ships' crews and the soldiers they carried, he would wager, were drones. The transport would be no threat at all to the *Hellhound* and easy targets to pick off when they were engaged. The drone soldiers they carried, though, would be the exact opposite when deployed on a planet's surface. If his gut was right, they would be designed to spread across a world like a virus, sweeping over it and consuming everything in their path.

The long-range scans had also very clearly detected the *Cerebus* on Ventari VII. That meant her cloak was down and she was already engaged with the enemy on some level. Hell didn't like her odds of survival as he weighed what he had deduced about the Kep'at's new alien allies given the amount of time the *Cerebus* had been alone down there. "Allies" was an overstatement. This new race would be better described as the Kep'at's new slaves. None the less, he didn't doubt their effectiveness as ground troops. The Kep'at wouldn't have bothered with using them if they weren't a force strong enough to change the balance of power in the war with the Alliance.

"Not lookin' good for our boys down there on the planet, is it, sir?" Major Page asked.

Colonel Hell pulled himself from the depths of his thoughts and turned his head to look at Page as he spoke, "No worse than usual." Hell's smile was sincere and wide.

Page laughed despite the circumstances or perhaps because of them.

"You're right on that one, Colonel," Page admitted, returning Hell's smile.

"The Kep'at presence in the Ventari system is formidable but not impenetrable," Hell said. "As yet, we have the advantage of surprise on our side. They can't know we're coming."

Hell returned to his thoughts for a moment and then addressed the *Hellhound*'s helmsman. "Drop us out of Void Space at these coordinates," he ordered.

The helmsman's eyes went wide. "That'll put us right on top of the Kep'at fleet stationed around the planet, sir."

"I am aware of that," Hell assured the man. "All weapon stations, be prepared to engage the enemy the instant we are clear of the Void."

"Yep," Major Page chuckled. "Just another day in the Banshees."

****

The number of tentacle-covered, humanoid creatures that had entered the *Cerebus* through the breach in her hangar bay was staggering. The things had kept pouring in, long after the bay's defenders were dead, right up until Lifeson had sacrificed his life in order to stop them and save Laybourne. Laybourne figured there were hundreds of the monsters left alive despite the efforts Lifeson made to stop them. The worst part of it was, the things were now free of the hangar area and into the ship itself. The last he had seen of the monsters, they had forced open one of the bay's lifts and were scurrying up its shaft.

Laybourne had tried numerous times to contact the bridge via the com-link of his combat helmet without success. Either it had gotten damage during the battle in the hangar bay or there was a problem with the *Cerebus*'s communications system. He hoped for the former but worried that the latter was true.

The ladder out of the maintenance compartment had continued lead upwards into the ship's top level decks, but he had gotten off it and entered a corridor on the deck just below the main bridge.

There he had found a few other Banshees under the command of Corporal Maria Felix. She and her fire team had been forced into retreat by the creatures. He could tell Maria was shaken but she was a professional and continued to act like one. She informed him that the creatures were indeed weapons of the Kep'at and were called Feeders. She also told him that the Kep'at had ordered Captain Pulliman to surrender and the captain had no intentions of doing so. Pulliman was even now desperately trying to get the ship moving despite the damage to her structural integrity. The captain planned to seal up those areas as best he could with energy fields and take the *Cerebus* into space. Laybourne knew things had to be *bad* if Pulliman was attempting the sort of escape he'd already told him was impossible. Still, if the captain thought their odds were better in space than on the planet's surface, that was his area and not his own. He trusted Pulliman's judgment even if it seemed like the last desperate act in attempting to keep them all alive that it most likely was.

Laybourne and Corporal Felix stood just behind the bend in the ship's corridor ahead of them. Felix's fire team was pouring it down on a pack of Feeders around the bend that were blocking their path.

"I agree," Felix shouted over the gunfire. "We need to head for the bridge but how?"

"We should be able to just fight our way through," Laybourne said. "The Feeders surely have to be spread out pretty widely across the ship by now!"

Felix shook her head. "I don't think that's the case, sir! We've been fighting a running battle with those things for a while now and anytime we try to head for the bridge, the resistance we encounter is always worse. It's like that's where the bulk of those things headed when they got out of the hangar bay!"

Laybourne frowned. He doubted the Kep'at could be controlling the Feeders through the ship's shields now that they were up. Of course, if the last command those things had gotten was "take the bridge," that did make sense.

"Okay," Laybourne admitted. "Maybe you're right but if they did head for the bridge, that's all the more reason for us to get there and as quickly as we can."

"One of my guys, well, he's my guy now at any rate, is a member of the ship's crew," she told him and then shouted, "Waters, get over here!"

A man wearing the uniform of a Banshee ensign left his position on the firing line at the bend in the corridor and came racing over to them.

"Ma'am?" He snapped to attention as he reached them.

"We need to get to the bridge, Waters," Felix barked at him. "And fast. Got any ideas?"

Waters fiddled with the data link he wore on his wrist. Every member of the *Cerebus* crew wore them. "I'm showing that some of the lifts are still functioning, ma'am. We could use one of those to at least get up to the bridge deck."

Laybourne's frown grew deeper. The Feeders were probably using the lift shafts as their primary method of getting around the ship. He didn't want to get stuck between floors with those things tearing at whatever lift they took, trying to get into it.

"The lifts aren't an option, ensign," Laybourne told him. "What else you got?"

****

No one on the bridge was expecting it when its main doors exploded inward. There was no explosion or blast that caused them to do so. They were simply torn down and flung out of the path of the stream of Feeders that came pouring onto the bridge in their wake.

Lieutenant Waid was the first to die. He was reaching for his sidearm as one of the monsters plowed into him, spearing his body with several of its tentacles. His screams became horrid gargling noises as his own blood welled up from his internal wounds and splashed outwards from his open mouth.

"Security to the bridge!" Captain Pulliman yelled but knew it was a futile act even as he uttered the words. If the Feeders had reached the bridge and gotten onto it, there likely wasn't any quick response team still alive close enough to aid them in time.

Gunshots rang out as those of his bridge crew that carried a sidearm tried to stem the tide of monsters flooding the bridge though its smashed doors. There was panic all around him as Ensign Anderson grabbed him by the arm and said, "This way, sir!"

Anderson dragged him into his ready room, just off the bridge. Its doors slid closed behind them just as a quartet of Feeders reached it. Pulliman could hear the monsters smashing their tentacles and primary hands against it in their rage. It took effort to collect his presence of mind enough to look at Anderson and say, "Thank you, Ensign."

"That door won't hold them long, sir," she warned him. "And I am not armed."

There was no standard requirement for Banshee naval personnel to carry side arms. Many did because they preferred to do so, especially when the ship was carrying a company of ground pounders like on this mission, but not all. Pulliman had never seen the need to do so himself. He was the captain and he figured if the time came he actually needed a handgun to defend himself with, the battle was already lost.

"Neither am I," Pulliman said, shoving by Anderson, to head for his desk.

The pounding on the ready room's door grew more intense. The metal was beginning to bend inward as he tried his private com-link. It was dead.

"We have to do something," Anderson kept her voice calm as she said the words. "We're Banshees, sir. I am not going to let those things rip me apart without a fight. They need to pay for every bit of flesh they take."

Pulliman walked over to the display case of swords on his ready room wall. There were three old Earth blades within it. He smashed out the glass covering them and tossed Anderson a short sword. She looked at him as if he were crazy.

"It's a lot better than your bare hands," he assured her, raising the long sword he'd taken for himself. It would be hard to use in such close quarters, much more so than the blade he had given Anderson, but he figured he could get in a few good swings.

"You ready?" he asked.

Anderson shook her head.

"Yeah." Pulliman laughed. "No one ever really is."

Then the door gave in under the Feeders' attack on it and the monsters came pouring in . . .

****

The corridor leading to the bridge was packed so thick with Feeders, the creatures themselves were having trouble moving. Their tentacles turned on each other in the packed space, rending flesh, as brother killed brother. Laybourne watched the sheer madness of their frenzy from a crawlspace in the corridor's roof at the far end from the bridge. There was only one means of clearing them all out that he could see. It was dangerous and stupid, but sometimes a Banshee had to do what a Banshee had to do.

"Pass me the belt," Laybourne ordered Corporal Maria Felix. She was next in line behind him in the narrow crawlspace. Behind her were Garth and Arron, the last two survivors of her fire team and those they had picked up and added to their group during their flight for the bridge. All the others were dead, lost in the battle on the deck below as they were forced to hold their ground long enough to make it into the ship's maintenance shafts.

Corporal Felix reluctantly handed the belt of grenades up to Laybourne. He took it from her and armed every grenade on it. He was only going to get one shot at this. When he opened the grill plating in front of him, the Feeders would know they were there. He knew the monsters would build a stack of their own corpses if they had to get at him and the others in the shaft. As thickly as the things were packed, that wouldn't take long either. Any kind of speedy retreat from their position was impossible. The Feeders would swarm up into the maintenance shaft and drag them out one by one to be fed upon. Even if Laybourne got his rifle into position inside the shaft to try to stop them, eventually, he would run out of ammo and the Feeders weren't going to give him a chance to reload.

His throw had to be spot on and perfect. *No pressure, right?* he thought as he double checked the belt of grenades making sure he had armed them all. The blast was going to be large one but that was the intent. The fact that it could possibly kill him, given his position, was a gamble he had no choice but to take if he and others had any hope of making it onto the bridge.

From where he was, Laybourne couldn't see the main doors of the bridge. The Feeders could have already broken through them and swarmed those inside. It didn't matter. He needed to reach the bridge in order to get an idea of how the ship overall was doing against the creatures. The things seemed to be everywhere, yes, but their numbers were limited and not the endless mass he and those in the hangar bay had faced before Captain Pulliman had gotten the *Cerebus*'s shields up. There was no indication that the shields weren't still up either. Every section he and those with him had fought their way through still had power. That meant that either the Feeders hadn't breached engineering yet or the Kep'at hadn't given them orders to do so once they were inside.

Taking a deep breath, Laybourne steeled himself and got ready to act. He silently counted to three in his head and then knocked the loosened grill plating into the corridor below. It dropped into the mass of Feeders. He only thought the creatures were in a frenzied state before. They went utterly wild as they spotted him and saw that they were not alone. Only their own numbers and the cramped space of the corridor kept them from managing to get up and get a hold on him before he was able to hurl the belt of grenades, over their heads, deep into their gathered mass near the entrance to the bridge.

As soon as the belt left his hand, Laybourne jerked himself back inside the shaft. A wave of white fire followed him as the corridor and shaft shook from the force of the explosion as the belt of grenades detonated. The wave of fire singed the hair on his exposed skin and set his sleeves ablaze. Laybourne cursed in pain as he beat out the fire on his arms that burned his flesh.

"Laybourne!" he heard Corporal Felix yelling at him. Her voice echoed in the shaft but even so sounded far away to his pain blurred mind. The blast had bent the shaft's opening upwards and Laybourne had to carefully angle his body over it as he readied himself to drop into the corridor below. He could see that the blast had decimated the Feeders. Feeder body parts and flaming remnants filled the space below him as he slid out of the shaft. His boots landed not on the solid metal flooring of the corridor but rather in a puddle of Feeder entrails and pus that stretched the length of the corridor. Here and there, a few of the things were still alive but they were so wounded, they were no immediate threat to him.

"I'm fine!" Laybourne yelled up at Felix and the others who were still in the shaft. "Get your butts down here, double time! This corridor won't stay clear for long!"

As Felix, Garth, and Arron followed him into the corridor, Laybourne stared at the seared undersides of his arms. They hurt like Hell. He longed for a medkit but neither he nor the others were carrying one.

Garth and Arron separated, each covering one end of the corridor, their rifle barrels raised and ready to meet any Feeders that came pouring towards them. Felix moved to Laybourne's side.

"Those are some pretty nasty burns, LT," she commented as she saw his arms. "We're going to need to do something about them."

"Later," Laybourne said, leaving no room for argument.

There was no sign of more Feeders coming as the four of them cautiously approached the entrance to the bridge with Garth on point.

"Oh frag it," Laybourne heard Garth mutter.

The doors leading onto the bridge were gone. The damage done to the frame they had rested in didn't look to have been caused by the blast either. Laybourne knew at once the Feeders had reached the bridge ahead of them despite their best efforts.

Garth picked up his pace as he neared the bridge's entrance, rushing to get onto it. In his haste, he got sloppy. A lone Feeder came tearing through the bridge's shattered doorway and caught him completely off guard. Garth tried to fire his rifle but one of the Feeder's tentacles was already wrapped around it. The monster jerked the rifle, sideways and up, as Garth fired. The rounds his weapon spat struck the corridor wall and then the ceiling, pinging off the metal they met there. Then with a twist, the Feeder yanked the weapon from Garth and flung it aside. Two more of its tentacles speared outwards stabbing Garth through his shoulders. They penetrated them entirely, emerging from their backsides, to curve around, reaching for Garth's throat. Garth got his pistol free of the holster on his hip and squeezed a trio of rounds into the Feeder's midsection. It grunted in pain and then snarled furiously as it pressed on into him, shoving Garth back into the corridor wall behind him. Both the Feeder and Garth lost their footing in the mess of Feeder bodies and fluids covering the corridor's floor. As they went down, the Feeder's face plunged forward, the teeth of its primary mouth tearing out Garth's throat in a spray of red.

Felix reacted before Laybourne. He blamed it on the pain he felt because he knew he was faster than she was. Her rifle came up and thundered next to him. A single, well aimed round blew apart the Feeder's head where it rose up over Garth's corpse.

Laybourne continued on towards the entrance to the bridge.

"Careful!" Corporal Felix warned him. "There could be more of those things in there."

Laybourne barely heard her words he was so focused on what lay ahead of him. He reached the open entrance to the bridge and stood staring into it. The bridge was just as grizzly a scene as the corridor he stood in. It was clear the bridge crew had been slaughtered quickly. Their ripped-apart, fed-upon bodies were everywhere. Only a couple of Feeder corpses rested with them. He walked onto the bridge, careful of where he stepped as he went, taking in the carnage.

"Our Father who art in Heaven, help us," he heard Corporal Felix praying.

"They didn't stand a chance," Arron commented and then dropped to one knee and added a puddle of vomit among the ones of blood.

"Get it together, Banshee," Laybourne growled at him.

Arron looked up at him with hard eyes. "I got it together, sir."

Laybourne nodded. "Corporal Felix, I want you to find out what you can about the state of the ship. The engineering station is over there." Laybourne pointed at it. "Arron, you watch that doorway."

"Yes, sir," the two of them chorused.

Laybourne left them to their jobs and approached Pulliman's ready room. Its door was battered in as well. Someone had made it into the room and tried to make a stand there. The Feeder corpses in the room were hacked up. At least three of them were missing their heads. One of them had an old Earth short sword buried in the center of its chest. Captain Pulliman's body, or rather what remained of it, was sprawled over the top of his deck, arms spread out wide, his chest torn open. Broken pieces of his ribs glinted white in the room's lighting, pointing up at its ceiling from where they had been wedged apart. Pulliman's insides looked to be picked clean. Blood dripped from the corners of the desk where he lay and Laybourne thought he could see bits of the man's spine through the bent back ribs of the open cavity that had been the captain's chest.

There was a female crew member in the room as well. Her clothes had been stripped and torn away but she was more than naked. Most of her flesh was gone. Whole sections of her bones were exposed where the monsters had feasted upon her and even they appeared to have been gnawed on.

Laybourne felt sick but he fought the feeling down, refusing to give into it as Arron had done. He paused to steady himself and then made the sign of the cross over his chest. He wasn't Catholic but had seen other Banshees do it and somehow it seemed the right thing to do in the moment. Laybourne turned his back on the mess in the ready room and headed back onto the bridge.

"Sir!" Corporal Felix called to him. "The *Cerebus* is lost. I ran scans of every deck as best I could and as far as I can tell, there aren't enough Banshees alive and still holding out to retake her.

It's just a matter of time until the Feeders will be all that's left on her."

Laybourne gave her an abrupt nod. "Is the internal comm functional?"

She blinked and then sprinted over to another bridge station, giving it a quick look-over. "I think so, sir."

"Give the order to abandon ship," he instructed her. "We're leaving."

****

The *Hellhound* lived up to her namesake as she emerged from Void Space and came all guns blazing into the Ventari system. The Kep'at battle fleet had no warning as she suddenly appeared and her forward missile launchers spat massive volleys at them. Two Kep'at destroyers took the brunt of that attack and blossomed into fireballs that flashed red and orange in the darkness of space. The *Hellhound*'s forward railgun emplacements hosed the rest of the Kep'at fleet, damaging a third destroyer so badly, it reeled sideways, careening into a fourth. The collusion sealed both of their fates. The *Hellhound* didn't let up as the Kep'at crews must have been racing towards their action stations and she continued to barrel down on them, her engines pushed to their limits.

One of the four Kep'at battleships in the system blocked her path to Ventari VII. All of the *Hellhound*'s weapon systems realigned to fire on it. The great ship's shields shuddered on the savageness of her attack and failed. A volley of missiles struck the battleship, followed by another at near point blank range for missile combat. The *Hellhound*'s own shields glowed as she rammed through the battleship's exploding wreckage, but they held. She sped onwards towards the planet but she wasn't done with the Kep'at fleet yet even so. Her aft launchers opened up, putting several more volleys of missiles hurling at the Kep'at fleet. A fifth and then a sixth Kep'at destroyer died in fire as they reached their targets. The volleys aimed at two of the Kep'at remaining three battleships were not as successful. One of the battleships took damage but not enough to render her ineffective. The other two managed last minute evasive maneuvers that quite probably kept them in the battle. Their captains managed to turn the great ships so that the missiles struck the best shielded and most armored sections.

The Kep'at battleships were indeed great ships. They were huge, well-armed, and almost the equal of an Alliance ship of their kind. They were not however "great" in comparison to the *Hellhound.* She was the only ship of her class. She had the size and firepower of a dreadnought but the speed and maneuverability of a much smaller vessel. Colonel Hell had spent a good deal of the fortune he had built up over the years making her into a killing machine without equal. She was easily more than a match for a small group of Kep'at battleships or even a Kep'at super dreadnought in a short fight where the advantage of surprise was on her side. Unfortunately, here in the Ventari system, she was on her own against an entire Kep'at battle fleet. If she tried to stand missile to missile with their numbers, she would be destroyed, though not quickly.

Colonel Hell appraised the damage she had done to the Kep'at battle fleet as she had rammed through its blockade around Ventari VII. Five destroyers and one battleship taken out was an impressive feat and he acknowledged it as such. However, it wasn't enough to matter in the long run. If the Kep'at fleet were able to properly engage her, the threat to the *Hellhound* would be immense.

The Kep'at fleet had finally managed to open fire on her. Missiles chased her across space as she continued her run for Ventari VII. EMC and her close in, defense batteries stopped the bulk of them but not all. The missiles that got through her defenses smashed into her shields, straining them.

"Shields are at fifty percent, sir, and falling!" Hell's tactical officer warned him.

There was no turning around now though. The *Hellhound* was committed to her course and the plan he had laid out for her during the trip to the Ventari system in Void Space.

"Engineering," Hell growled, "Get me more speed!"

Hell closed the channel before his chief engineer could reply. Whatever the woman said, it didn't matter. Either she would manage to do it or not. Hell was well aware that the engines were at their limits already but when push came to shove, you found a way or paid the price for it.

"The Kep'at fleet is pursuing us, sir!" a bridge officer informed him. "Missiles inbound!"

"Count?" Hell snapped.

"Best estimate, over one hundred, sir!"

That meant every single one of the cursed Kep'at ships had emptied their tubes at the *Hellhound* in an attempt to damage her and slow her down before she reached Ventari VII. He had to admit that he would have ordered the same if he were in command of the Kep'at fleet but being on the receiving end of such an order didn't mean he had to like it.

"Reroute all available power that isn't being dumped into the engines into the aft shields!" Hell shouted.

Missile after missile slammed into the *Hellhound.* So far, the shields were continuing to hold but Colonel Hell knew that wouldn't last.

"Open a channel to the *Cerebus!"* Hell ordered. "Tell her to get airborne and into space, now! Combat landing is approved!"

The *Cerebus* was a large ship in her right but she was nothing compared to the mass of the *Hellhound.* It carried three more ships like her in its bays. Still, the *Cerebus* wasn't an agile, little fighter either. A combat landing for a ship her size came with a good deal of risk but it was the only option. The *Hellhound*'s shields were in no shape to be extended around her so bringing her in and fast was the only means of ensuring the Kep'at fleet didn't reduce her to chunks of drifting metal as soon as she cleared Ventari VII's atmosphere.

"No reply from the *Cerebus,* Colonel!" Hell's comm officer shouted at him, the man's nerves were clearly frayed and his worried expression made his twisted face appear almost comical to Hell.

"Hail her again!" Colonel Hell ordered. "And keep trying until you get a reply!"

"Yes, sir!" the comm officer snapped.

Major Page stood watching it all beside where Colonel Hell sat in his command chair.

"This isn't going exactly to plan," he commented.

"Does it ever?" Hell fluffed off the concern in Page's voice. "There's no reason to worry . . . yet."

Hell craned his neck to look at Page. "If we don't make contact with the *Cerebus* and pick her up by the time we reached Ventari VII, we'll have to write her off, yes, but we'll be able to slingshot around the planet and bloody the nose of that fleet behind us one more time before we FTL the Hades out of here."

"Sounds like you're giving up?" Page snorted.

"No," Hell replied, "I'm being practical like always. We may lose the pay for completing our original mission but I'll make damn sure the Alliance pays us for our loses and use the damage we have done to the Kep'at here to ensure that we get it."

The bridge shook, causing Major Page to stumble. He kept his feet though and quickly regained his balance.

"They may owe us a lot by the time all this plays out," Page complained.

Hell said nothing, his gaze fixed on the growing dot of Ventari VII on the bridge's forward view screen.

****

Laybourne, Corporal Felix, and Private Willie Arron strapped themselves into the seats of the attack craft. It was one of two the *Cerebus* carried in her hangar bay. The other had been all but destroyed during the battle in the bay Laybourne had been a part of earlier.

Making it to the bay hadn't been as difficult as Laybourne feared it would be when he led the others off the ship's bridge. They had spent the better part of the last hour navigating the network of maintenance shafts that ran through the *Cerebus*'s bulkheads. Their encounters with the Feeders getting to the hangar bay had been nothing more than a few brief skirmishes. The Feeders were spread out all over the *Cerebus* now, wandering her corridors in small packs, searching for prey. Laybourne suspected that once the order the creatures had been given by their Kep'at masters, in regards to taking out the ship's bridge, was completed, the things had reverted to nothing more than hungry drones. All that mattered to them was once again finding a means to feed the hunger that was a part of what they were.

Laybourne knew that he and the others were lucky the find the second attack craft still intact and functional. Private Arron had strapped into its rear while Corporal Felix took the co-pilot seat next to him.

"You know how to fly one of these things?" she asked as she snapped the last belt of her the safety harness securing her into place.

With a shrug, Laybourne laughed. "How hard could it be?"

"Oh Hell no!" he heard Arron yell from the attack craft's rear section. "You don't have a clue, do you?"

Arron quickly added the word "sir" to his question as Laybourne turned to glare over his shoulder at him.

"You can stay here with the monsters if you want, Banshee," Laybourne offered, "but I wouldn't advise it."

Arron shut his mouth and finished strapping in.

Laybourne eyed the controls in front of him, and through luck more than skill, managed to power up the attack craft. Its engines whined to life.

"Here goes everything," he said to Corporal Felix as he bent over the controls and concentrated his full attention on them.

The ship took off . . . shooting backwards as it lifted from the floor of the deck to bang against the bulkhead of the hangar bay. Sparks fell as metal met metal. Laybourne and the others were shaken about in their seats but the collusion didn't appear to do any real damage to the attack craft.

"Sir!" Corporal Felix snapped at him. "The breach in the hull you're aiming for is that way!"

She flung an arm out, extending a finger to point at the breach.

"I got it!" Laybourne told her.

The expression she wore was more than a little doubtful.

"I really do this time," he assured her.

"You better make sure the *Cerebus*'s shields aren't still sealing that breach!" Private Arron shouted.

Corporal Felix nodded her agreement. "That sounds like a really good idea to me too, sir."

Laybourne looked over the controls in front of him. He spotted the ones for the attack craft's forward guns and engaged them as he brought the ship around to face the breach. High-velocity rounds sprayed from the attack craft's wing mounted weapon emplacements. The shield was still up. It crackled and glowed as the rounds slammed into it. Ricochets bounced through the hangar bay, some striking the attack craft's own forward hull. Laybourne winced as they did so.

"Sorry," he said as he killed the stream of fire from the attack craft's weapons.

"Put up our blasted shields first next time, sir," Felix ordered him despite her lower rank. "Nevermind," she added, flicking a switch on the console. "I'll do it for you."

"Thanks," Laybourne said sincerely.

"That shield held," she told him. "You're going to have to blast it again."

Laybourne nodded and engaged the attack craft's weapons a second time. Rounds bounced off the shield once more but this time he didn't let up. None of the ricochets were getting through the attack craft's own shields. The shield covering the breach began to shimmer and finally collapsed under the constant barrage Laybourne poured into it. It flicked out of existence and the spray of rounds streamed through the breach into the air outside of it.

"You did it, sir!" Corporal Felix cried, leaning over to place one of her hands atop one of his.

Laybourne smiled at her.

She quickly jerked her hand away from his and resumed her professional, if frazzled, manner.

"And away we go!" Laybourne exclaimed as he kicked the attack craft's engines up a notch and the ship darted through the breach, leaving the *Cerebus* and her hangar bay behind it.

****

"Colonel!" the sensor tech on the *Hellhound*'s bridge shouted at him. "I've got a Banshee attack craft on my screen. It's lifting from the surface of Ventari VII and should break atmosphere within the next minute."

"It's responding to our hails!" the comm officer added. "It's First Lieutenant Laybourne Colonel. He's requesting to come aboard!"

"Combat landing!" Colonel Hell snapped wondering if his earlier orders had been forgotten in the excitement of detecting the Banshee attack craft in route for them.

The Kep'at fleet remained in pursuit of the *Hellhound* and continued to pound her with everything it had. Her shields were barely holding on. The last report Hell heard put that at eight percent. *It'll be enough,* he thought to himself as he flashed a wicked smile.

The small attack craft First Lieutenant Laybourne was bringing in was shielded from the main fire of the Kep'at fleet by the *Hellhound.* Laybourne should have no problem getting her into the giant ship's hangar except for the fact that he wasn't a pilot. That was a variable that even Hell's almost supernatural intuition couldn't predict the outcome of.

The *Hellhound* shook as yet another wave of Kep'at missiles hammered her weakened shields.

"Deck 7 and 12 are venting atmosphere," his tactical officer reported.

The ship had taken her fair share of damage under the Kep'at's continued, relentless attacks but so far, all her major systems were online and still functioning. That was a good thing because they were going to need them as soon as Laybourne's attack craft was onboard.

The bridge fell silent as Hell gave the order, "Slow us down."

No one argued though. It was a testament to their faith in him as the *Hellhound* slowed to take better Laybourne's chance of surviving the attack craft's landing in her hangar bay. The *Hellhound* rocked as she stopped her evasive spin to pick up Laybourne. Her shields finally failed but her armor held.

Major Page looked on the verge of being sick to Colonel Hell. Hell couldn't blame the man. The major was a ground pounder and unaccustomed being as helpless as he was now in regard to his own fate.

"The First Lieutenant is aboard, sir!"

"Slingshot us around Ventari VII now!" Hell screamed at his helmsman.

The giant ship swerved around the outer edge of the planet's gravitational pull and came about to streak towards the Kep'at battle fleet at near light speed.

Colonel Hell grasped the ends of the arms of his command chair so tightly his knuckles popped. "All weapons, fire at will!"

The *Hellhound*'s forward launchers emptied their tubes and her railguns blazed. The Kep'at formation chasing her broke apart as the commanders of its ships scrambled to dodge what they could of the unexpected, incoming fire.

A Kep'at battleship crumbled under a volley of her missiles. Pieces of its hull spun away into the void as it broke apart. The *Hellhound*'s railguns battered a trio of spread-out Kep'at destroyers as she approached them and then sped on past them. Her streams of fire turned one destroyer into a ball of erupting fire and shrapnel before turning to slice one of the destroyers along its entire length, gutting the ship, and leaving it drifting and venting atmosphere.

Then she was through the Kep'at formation and quickly leaving it behind. To their credit, the commanders of the Kep'at vessels were trying hard to bring their ships around and come after her as Hell gave the order, "Spin up the FTL drive. Prepare to jump on my mark."

Hell wasn't quite ready to bug out yet. The primitive transports the Kep'at had carried their new shock troops to Ventari VII sat unguarded in the *Hellhound*'s path. Leaving them as thus showed the Kep'at overconfidence and Hell was going to make sure the bastards paid dearly for it. A fierce grin spread his lips and he almost licked them at the sight of them.

"All batteries, target those transports. I want them burnt out of the sky," he ordered.

The primitive vessels, even with the Kep'at tech upgrades they had received, disintegrated under a short burst of fire from the *Hellhound*. Cheers of victory rang out all across her bridge.

Half a minute later, as the Kep'at fleet had finally came about enough to open fire at the *Hellhound* again, Hell very calmly said, "Jump", as a wide smile stretched across the bird-like features of his face.

The *Hellhound* flashed and then was gone.

****

Two weeks later. . .

Laybourne was still getting used to being addressed by the rank of Major. Colonel Hell had given him the promotion himself after the events of Ventari VII. The colonel didn't seem to care that he lost an entire company and the *Cerebus* in the process. Laybourne knew that was because of the substantial bonus the Alliance had given Colonel Hell for not only bringing them the data they wanted on the Kep'at new race of Feeder combat drones but also the number of Kep'at ships the *Hellhound* had taken out in the process.

The dropship rattled around Major Alex Laybourne as it descended into the atmosphere of Reitta XII. The Kep'at hadn't given up their push into Alliance space despite the setbacks of Ventari VILL. Reitta XII was the latest world to come under attack by their new Feeders.

Laybourne glanced over at newly promoted Lieutenant Felix. She returned the smile he gave her. The two of them had hooked up and became something of an item these days. *The Banshees that kill together, stay together,* Laybourne thought to himself and laughed.

Soon the dropship's door would blow and the battle would start but he didn't care. This was his home and he was glad to be here.

THE END

Eric S Brown is author of numerous series including the Bigfoot War series, the Crypto-Squad series (with Jason Brannon), the Kaiju Apocalypse series (with Jason Cordova), The Homeworld series, The "A Pack of Wolves" series, and the Jack Bunny Bam-Bam series. Some of his stand alone books include Kraken, Megalodon, Megalodons, Megalodon Apocalypse, War of the World Plus Blood Guts and Zombies, Sasquatch Lake, Crawlers, Season of Rot, and Kaiju Armageddon to name only a few. His short fiction has been published hundreds of times in the small press and beyond including markets like Baen Books' Onward Drake and Black Tide Rising anthologies, the Grantville Gazette, Walmart World Magazine, and the SNAFU anthology series. He has written the novelizations for such films as Boggy Creek: The Legend is True and The Bloody Rage of Bigfoot. Two of his own books have been adapted into feature films the first of which was Bigfoot War in 2014 by Origin Releasing. Eric also writes an ongoing comic book news column entitled "Comics in a Flash." He lives in North Carolina with his wife and two children where he continues to write tales of blazing guns, hungry corpses, and the monsters that lurk in the woods.

CHECK OUT OTHER GREAT SCIENCE FICTION BOOKS

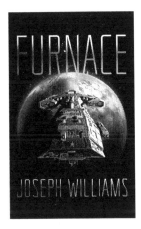

FURNACE
by Joseph Williams

On a routine escort mission to a human colony, Lieutenant Michael Chalmers is pulled out of hyper-sleep a month early. The RSA Rockne Hummel is well off course and—as the ship's navigator—it's up to him to figure out why. It's supposed to be a simple fix, but when he attempts to identify their position in the known universe, nothing registers on his scans. The vessel has catapulted beyond the reach of starlight by at least a hundred trillion light-years. Then a planetary-mass object materializes behind them. It's burning brightly even without a star to heat it. Hundreds of damaged ships are locked in its orbit. The crew discovers there are no life-signs aboard any of them. As system failures sweep through the Hummel, neither Chalmers nor the pilot can prevent the vessel from crashing into the surface near a mysterious ancient city. And that's where the real nightmare begins.

LUNA
by Rick Chesler

On the threshold of opening the moon to tourist excursions, a private space firm owned by a visionary billionaire takes a team of non-astronauts to the lunar surface. To address concerns that the moon's barren rock may not hold long-term allure for an uber-wealthy clientele, the company's charismatic owner reveals to the group the ultimate discovery: life on the moon.

But what is initially a triumphant and world-changing moment soon gives way to unrelenting terror as the team experiences firsthand that despite their technological prowess, the moon still holds many secrets.

CHECK OUT OTHER GREAT SCIENCE FICTION BOOKS

IN PERPETUITY
by Jake Bible

For two thousand years, Earth and her many colonies across the galaxy have fought against the Estelian menace. Having faced overwhelming losses, the CSC has instituted the largest military draft ever, conscripting millions into the battle against the aliens. Major Bartram North has been tasked with the unenviable task of coordinating the military education of hundreds of thousands of recruits and turning them into troops ready to fight and die for the cause.

As Major North struggles to maintain a training pace that the CSC insists upon, he realizes something isn't right on the Perpetuity. But before he can investigate, the station dissolves into madness brought on by the physical booster known as pharma. Unfortunately for Major North, that is not the only nightmare he faces- an armada of Estelian warships is on the edge of the solar system and headed right for Earth!

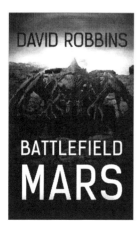

BATTLEFIELD MARS
by David Robbins

Several centuries into the future, Earth has established three colonies on Mars. No indigenous life has been discovered, and humankind looks forward to making the Red Planet their own.

Then 'something' emerges out of a long-extinct volcano and doesn't like what the humans are doing.

Captain Archard Rahn, United Nations Interplanetary Corps, tries to stem the rising tide of slaughter. But the Martians are more than they seem, and it isn't long before Mars erupts in all-out war.

CHECK OUT OTHER GREAT SCIENCE FICTION BOOKS

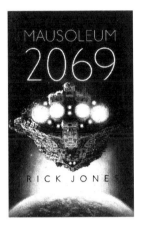

MAUSOLEUM 2069
by Rick Jones

Political dignitaries including the President of the Federation gather for a ceremony onboard Mausoleum 2069. But when a cloud of interstellar dust passes through the galaxy and eclipses Earth, the tenants within the walls of Mausoleum 2069 are reborn and the undead begin to rise. As the struggle between life and death onboard the mausoleum develops, Eriq Wyman, a one-time member of a Special ops team called the Force Elite, is given the task to lead the President to the safety of Earth. But is Earth like Mausoleum 2069? A landscape of the living dead? Has the war of the Apocalypse finally begun? With so many questions there is only one certainty: in space there is nowhere to run and nowhere to hide.

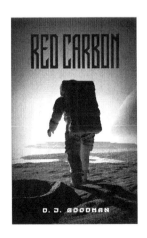

RED CARBON
by D.J. Goodman

Diamonds have been discovered on Mars.

After years of neglect to space programs around the world, a ruthless corporation has made it to the Red Planet first, establishing their own mining operation with its own rules and laws, its own class system, and little oversight from Earth. Conditions are harsh, but its people have learned how to make the Martian colony home.

But something has gone catastrophically wrong on Earth. As the colony leaders try to cover it up, hacker Leah Hartnup is getting suspicious. Her boundless curiosity will lead her to a horrifying truth: they are cut off, possibly forever. There are no more supplies coming. There will be no more support. There is no more mission to accomplish. All that's left is one goal: survival.

CHECK OUT OTHER GREAT
SCIENCE FICTION BOOKS

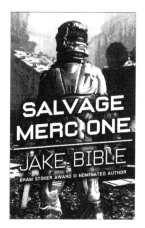

SALVAGE MERC ONE
by Jake Bible

Joseph Laribeau was born to be a Marine in the Galactic Fleet. He was born to fight the alien enemies known as the Skrang Alliance and travel the galaxy doing his duty as a Marine Sergeant. But when the War ended and Joe found himself medically discharged, the best job ever was over and he never thought he'd find his way again.

Then a beautiful alien walked into his life and offered him a chance at something even greater than the Fleet, a chance to serve with the Salvage Merc Corp.

Now known as Salvage Merc One Eighty-Four, Joe Laribeau is given the ultimate assignment by the SMC bosses. To his surprise it is neither a military nor a corporate salvage. Rather, Joe has to risk his life for one of his own. He has to find and bring back the legend that started the Corp.

SERENGETI
by J.B. Rockwell

It was supposed to be an easy job: find the Dark Star Revolution Starships, destroy them, and go home. But a booby-trapped vessel decimates the Meridian Alliance fleet, leaving Serengeti—a Valkyrie class warship with a sentient AI brain—on her own; wrecked and abandoned in an empty expanse of space. On the edge of total failure, Serengeti thinks only of her crew. She herds the survivors into a lifeboat, intending to sling them into space. But the escape pod sticks in her belly, locking the cryogenically frozen crew inside.

Then a scavenger ship arrives to pick Serengeti's bones clean. Her engines dead, her guns long silenced, Serengeti and her last two robots must find a way to fight the scavengers off and save the crew trapped inside her.

Made in the USA
San Bernardino, CA
25 May 2017